ISBN-13: 979-8-9893928-0-3

Cover design by: Coverjig
Library of Congress Control Number: 2018675309
Printed in the United States of America

*For BlackSheep ~ for whom this story would
have never made it into the light.*

Contents

Useful Info/Terms

- <u>Romanian Forest:</u> The Romanian forest is a dense and ancient woodland, characterized by towering trees and a thick undergrowth. The forest stretches for miles, creating a vast and mysterious landscape. It is home to an abundance of flora and fauna, with various species of plants and animals thriving within its boundaries.

- <u>Loup Garou Packs:</u> Within the depths of the Romanian forest, several packs of Loup-Garous have established their territories. These supernatural creatures, also known as werewolves, live in close-knit communities within the forest. They have adapted to their surroundings, utilizing the dense vegetation and natural features of the forest to their advantage.

- <u>Human Towns:</u> Just outside the woods, towns have been established by humans.These towns serve as a hub for trade, commerce, and interaction to fuel the growth of the human population that are unaware of the creatures the inhabit just inside the forests.

- <u>Enchanted Glades:</u> Scattered throughout the Romanian forest are enchanting glades, hidden pockets of magic where the boundaries between the mortal world and the supernatural realm are thin. These glades are filled with vibrant flowers, sparkling streams, and ethereal creatures. They hold a mystical energy.

- <u>Mysterious Caves:</u> The forest is also dotted with numerous caves, some of which hold ancient secrets and treasures. These caves are shrouded in mystery, with winding passages and hidden chambers that lead to unknown depths. Many believe that these caves hold the key to long-forgotten knowledge of the forest's history.

- <u>Seasonal Changes:</u> The Romanian forest experiences distinct seasonal changes, each bringing its own unique charm. In the spring, the forest comes alive with vibrant blossoms and fresh growth. Summer brings warmth and a symphony of chirping birds and buzzing insects. Autumn paints the forest in shades of gold, red, and orange as the leaves change, while winter covers the landscape in a blanket of snow, transforming it into a magical winter wonderland.

Unu

No one in his small community kept any doors locked. It was an insult to lock your doors to the family. They were all welcome in any home and welcome to whatever was in it.

"Dad?" Micah called as he walked through the front door after taking his afternoon run, but he got nothing. That was odd, his father was usually home at this time. Micah listened and heard footsteps coming near him.

"Your father took off with a couple of other hunters."

Just great, that meant that he wasn't going to be home for a few hours if not tomorrow. But he shrugged it off and turned to leave.

"Can I help, sweetie?" Micah turned around to his mother.

"No, not really. Just something I needed to talk to him about," he replied, and she meekly nodded her head.

"Alright. Stay safe, " she told him, and he left the house once more.

Micah made his way through the small village of sorts, greeting people here and there and playing with the kids that were running around for a little bit. But as he got further and further away from everyone, he closed his eyes and used his other senses to see where he was going. As he walked through the dense forest, a scent came to him. It smelled familiar, and something in him screamed at him to dominate, possess, and take what is his. This had never happened to him, but he was aware of what it was. Apparently, he wouldn't need to talk to his father. The scent led him through the forest and to the one that would be his. He knew that his father would be pleased if this turned out well. For the moon would be full, and his time would be up to find his mate, and then he wouldn't be able to succeed his father unless a challenge was made.

Micah followed his senses to town and then opened his eyes, looking around. Trying to narrow down who he was supposed to be finding. That was until his eyes landed on a particular female. He reeled back when he felt like pouncing on the girl. This had to be some kind of mistake. This was a human. Micah's eyes tracked the female to make sure that it was supposed to be this person, and when he couldn't tear his gaze from the woman, he knew that it was right. The only problem with this - no Alpha in his pack had ever had any other mate than a Loup Garou.

He took several deep breaths and felt himself losing the battle within himself.

"Mic! What the hell are you doing?" Micah heard someone call out to him, and that's when he definitely freaked out.

"Dammit, Jonny. Don't sneak up on me like that, and shhh," he yelled and then dropped his voice.

"Me sneak up on you? That's odd, I haven't been able to do that since we were pups. Wait, why was I able to now?" The young male's thoughts bounced around so quickly, but Micah was able to keep up. He quickly wrapped a hand around the guy's mouth.

"Shut up," he growled at him and looked back quickly, hoping that the girl hadn't heard anything.

Micah quickly pulled Jonny away from what he assumed was the college campus before they were caught, and then he released him.

"What the hell was that all about?" Jonny protested once he was able to talk.

"I was stalking my prey, and you just ruined it for me," he yelled the first thing that popped into his head at the guy.

"A human? But your father made it clear that we can not hunt humans."

Micah swung a hand out at Johnny, and he ducked. "I don't care what my father says. I will be pack leader soon so I can do what I want when I want, and if you breathe a word of this, then I will make sure you pay. Got it. " He gripped the guy's collar, pulling him up to meet his eyes. Jonny gulped loudly and nodded his head in agreement.

"Good now, get back to the village." Micah dropped him and watched as his pack mate stalked off home.

Micah turned back around to the human, thankful that she hadn't gotten too far away, and looked around. The place was pleasantly sparse of other humans. 'Can't wait any longer,' he thought to himself and made his move. Micah moved with blinding speed and precision, up to the human. Standing in front of her, his height was well above hers and forced the woman to stop on the path. "You'll be coming with me," Micah ordered the girl. However, he didn't give her any amount of time to think about the situation and picked the girl up to sling her over his shoulder. Micah quickly glanced around once more and then took off before he got caught.

~*~*~

Miya sighed as the professor finally released the class for the weekend, and she sighed heavily as she made her way from the lecture. It wouldn't have been so bad if it was just a lecture, but there was an hour-long demonstration as well. She made a quick stop at the locker rooms so that she could change out of her scrubs and locked it all up. Her locker housed her extra scrubs, along with some textbooks. If someone even peeked into her locker, they would find it well organized and neat. This was not because she wanted it to be that way, but a habit that was drilled into her by her father. Once she changed back into her black and white t-shirt and pale blue jeans, she started off for the residential buildings. After all, it was best to get homework out of the way when it was still fresh in her mind. It wasn't like she had anything else to do this weekend. Her social circle was small...well, non-existent, really.

As she wandered her way through the courtyard, she would close her eyes every so often to enjoy the sunshine and breathe in the fresh air. It felt good to finally have the freedom that college life advertised, and she savored every moment of it. When she first got to the college campus, she was stupid and became a party girl just because she could, but soon buckled down into studies after she got her first D. Her mind brought up the memory and was thankful that her parents hadn't found out about it before she could fix the mistake.

Miya smiled as she walked past the daycare and watched the little ones running around like crazed animals. Watching the children also reminded her of how happy she was to be far, far away from her mother and her match-making. Miya never really had the heart to tell her parents that she wasn't interested in having children of her own. The thought of having to take care of another being just wasn't in the cards for her. Nope. She just wanted to save the lives that were already here on this planet. She was afraid that if her parents ever found out that she just wanted a career instead of a family, her mother would go nuts and probably drag her home by her ear...she shuddered at the thought.

The college she got into was in a nice town, slowly growing larger with each year. Miya wouldn't be surprised if it turned into a major city in the near future. Her dark steel eyes looked around, taking in the sights until she saw a man standing near the forest's edge, just looking at her. At first, she had the urge to turn and walk back towards the bustling main street, but with a second glance, the man seemed to be acting oddly. *'Is he having an attack of some kind?'* She thought because it looked like the guy was trying to calm himself down or something. Miya knew that it was probably a bad idea to just walk up to a strange man, but if he was in trouble, she couldn't help herself. She just had to help, it was her nature. She took a step in the direction of the man, but as someone came up behind the man, she decided to just continue on her way. It looked like whoever he was waiting for came calling out the man's name.

She was happily on her way back towards the residential buildings and getting pretty far from the two strange men, even forgetting about the creeping feeling she had experienced not a few minutes ago. Her bag dug into her shoulders a little more with each step, reminding her how much work she had to do. Miya slightly picked up her pace in an effort to get back to her apartment before her bag cut off all circulation to her arm.

However, to her surprise, she saw the man she thought was having an attack early, and he was suddenly in front of her. She had to look up quite a lot just to see the man's face which made her neck hurt. As soon as the man ordered her that she would be going with him, Miya was about to snap at the guy, but she was picked up! This fucking brute just swung her over his shoulder like she was a sack of feathers. When the man started to move towards the forest she had no other thought and started yelling. Her hands dug into the man's back hoping that she could get the man to stop long enough for a knee to the balls. "Let me down RIGHT NOW!" She yelled and wiggled in the guy's grip as much as she could while throwing punches every which way. Like hell she was going to go willingly and she hoped someone would hear her before she was taken too far. Miya even went so far as to elbow the guy as hard as she could in the back of the head. Any lesser man would have been out cold with that. Miya was by no means a weakling or pushover. Her father made sure that she was prepared for anything that life could possibly throw at her. Unfortunately, nothing worked in her favor.

Doi

He was thankful that he was fast. However, he could have done without the screaming coming from the woman. It wasn't like he had torn the girl's torso apart right there on the street. Well, to be fair, she didn't know what he was, and at the moment, that was a good thing. He sighed lightly as he trekked closer to the forest, thoughts drifting in and out of his head. The annoyance of the scratches was starting to get to him, though it was the elbow to the back of the head that broke through to him.

Micah jerked the girl into the air briefly before letting her land back down on his shoulder, effectively stunning the human, and he continued walking. "Would you just be quiet for a moment and you can stop flailing around like that, it ain't gonna do much" Micah explained to the woman over her screams and futile attempts to bash his head again.

As much as Micah would have liked to take the girl back to his house and place her in his room until he knew exactly what he was going to do, he knew that was not an option. At least not until he could talk to his father, but then again, he couldn't exactly let the woman go free either. If she got too far away because he let her go or just randomly disappeared from the city, Micah would go nuts. With the moon almost full and his heat not too far behind that, he knew that he would hunt her down in his fur, and that would surely ruin things.

Micah could hear the laughter and soft yips of pups playing out in the courtyard along with idle chit-chat coming from the adults that littered about the houses and courtyards. From this point, he changed directions, so he was walking away from the village and started to head into the darker parts of the woods where only his father and the hunters went. Micah was banking on the information that his mother had given to him earlier, that his father was out with a few of the hunting groups, and that he wouldn't be back for quite some time.

When he could no longer hear the sound of the others at home Micah stopped for a few seconds to scan the area, making sure there was nothing or no one that would get in his way right now. Deeming the area safe, Micah bound up the side of a small, well to him, mountainside and stopped at the closest ledge to the ground. However, that close ledge was still a good twenty feet off the ground. He finally felt safe enough to slide the girl from his shoulder, effectively dropping her on her ass in as much of a gentle way that he could and took a deep breath. He held his breath for a moment before releasing the trapped air with a loud annoyed hiss.

~*~*~

She yelped when the guy jerked her into the air, and her eyes widened in shock. Miya huffed as the breath from her lungs was knocked from her. She was stunned for a bit, but once she got her head back she dug her nails into the man's shirt in a small attempt to cause the guy pain and not to focus on her own pain. Miya cursed under her breath, calling the guy every name in the book that she could think of, but in all honesty, she was scared out of her mind. What could this guy possibly want with her? Other than the obvious, which she was trying her hardest not to think about. She wasn't rich or famous. Maybe he was a deranged serial killer, and she was his next victim. That thought caused the blood to drain from her face.

Miya took a few deep breaths to calm down. She tilted her head to the side to see if she recognized anything. She got worried, noticing that they were deep in the forest. A part that she hadn't dared to venture. It would be hard for any search parties to track her here, but if she could hold out, she could use her cell phone to call for help the first chance she got. She hoped the guy wouldn't kill her once they stopped. After all, Miya never did anything to piss someone off enough to kill her, or she at least hoped not. "Is there a rest stop between here and whatever imaginary place you are taking me to?" She growled out, finally finding her sarcastic wit she usually used when she was nervous or scared.

At one point, she thought she could hear people, or it could have just been random noises in the wind, but it was much too far off for her to really hear with her normal hearing. Miya wiggled some more, hoping she could slip from the guy's vice like hold. The man's shoulder was digging painfully into her abdomen and was becoming quite unconformable. Her black hair had fallen from its tie to drape over her shoulders, but she could still see that they had moved into a much darker part of the forest. Yeah, this was not a good sign.

She felt the man stop for a moment, giving her a better chance to look around, but she realized that she was completely lost in the woods. There were times Miya walked around the forest to de-stress, but not that often. After all, she was going into a medical field, and studying was a must if Miya wanted to keep up her good grades.

She was shocked when the guy jumped up a mountain, and when they got to the ledge, she was unceremoniously dropped. Miya didn't wait another second longer and jumped to her feet to move as far away from the man as she could while glaring at him murderously. If she had the time, she could pull out something from her bag to use as a weapon. A pencil or pen possibly and get a good stab or two into the guy. She waited with baited breath as the man didn't say anything when taking a deep breath and sighed it out. She just needed to wait. The guy looked like he could overpower her. Miya had to be smart so she could make the right decision. Just like chess.

"So what's the plan now, genius?" She snapped in response to his hiss of air and probably digging a deeper hole for herself but she was having a hard time keeping her mouth shut since she was trying not to have a full breakdown right now.

Trei

He took a deep breath, staring out at the tops of the trees, well, at least the smaller ones, since they weren't up high enough to see over the taller trees. "Right now the details of any plan are not necessary for you. So I suggest you get comfortable, and quick." Micah told her with a matter of fact tone that left no room for argument. However, by the way this woman moved and snapped that she would try anyway, but it would end badly either way the girl tried.

There was a sense of longing and attachment Micah had for her already, the pull to his mate was something that he could not and would not ignore. Thus, he finally turned to look at her. His eyes softened a little but because it wasn't something he was used to, he probably still looked like he was glaring. "There are things that happen that can't be changed and I'm not about to go against this pull. I...I guess you humans would say I'm feeling guilty for what I just did to you, but guilt really isn't something I feel. Wasn't raised that way..." Micah started to tell her, but he wasn't even sure if his words were coming across the right way.

Micah ran a hand through his short hair, tugging slightly, hoping to square out his thoughts. "What I'm trying to say is, that one in my position doesn't normally find their mate in a human. Granted, it's not unheard of for others, but not ones like me and, by some twisted fate, that is what has happened today."

Micah guessed right that Miya would fight every step of the way. After all, she had no idea what the guy wanted in the first place. She was worried as she glanced over the side of the ledge to see if she could get down at all, maybe even jump over to the trees and climb down to get the hell away from this guy. "Yeah, because that's a good way to calm down your victims. Really, they should give you an award." Miya said, making sure she was far from the guy's reach, and slowly started to dig into her backpack. She needed to find something she could use to defend herself with.

When the guy finally turned towards her, she was confused. She didn't understand why the man was glaring at her but she glared right back until he started talking about fate and a pull. This guy even had the gall to call her human like he wasn't one himself. "Want to know a way to get rid of guilt? Let me go and we can act like this never happened. I won't call the cops and have you locked up in a loony bin and you can go off and do whatever crazy people do," she said, just as her hand felt a pen at the bottom of her bag. Miya slowly pulled the pen from her bag, making sure it was hidden from the guys' view by using her water bottle that she pulled out with the pen.

Miya tilted her head in thought, the words mate, human and fate finally clicking in her head. Those simple words made her think of wild ideas but she didn't voice them. "What do you mean mate?" Maybe the guy was British? Or was he talking about the sexual kind of mate? She was willing to jump if things got out of hand. She just hoped that she wouldn't break anything on the landing.

Micah smirked at the bite of the girl's words, at least she seemed like she would be a challenge for him. He would be pissed if fate had paired him with some kind of wimpy crybaby that he would rather slaughter then mate with. He wondered just what to do with this girl. Micah sniffed the air a little bit to ease his suspicions before dropping his tense shoulders. He wasn't sure whether he should be angry that this woman didn't feel the same as him or laugh at her words. However, as the girl continued to talk and started to shift around inside her bag, Micah couldn't help but bust out laughing. His stomach clenched a bit, making him wrap an arm around his abdomen before taking a deep breath to get himself back under control.

"Whew, alright, I'm starting to see a bit more why this happened." Micah finally said when he was able to breath and talk normally again. "I guess since I've already mixed things up..." Micah gently held his hand out, however realized that was probably a bad idea with someone this jumpy and snippy. So, instead, he pulled his hand back and ran it through his hair before letting it rest on the back of his neck. "My name's Micah and you are my mate...er soulmate, lover, whatever you humans call it..." Micah explained as he thought about it and then the word popped into his head "I got it. You guys say wife" he exclaimed softly.

It wasn't that he wasn't versed in human ways, but forgetting their customs was more likely with Micah, only because he didn't care to remember them or acknowledge them. The only times he had to deal with the humans was if they needed some supplies that they couldn't hunt for. His father had tried to make sure they stayed like that so no one in the pack would become too dependent on the human race, because then that would lead to slip-ups and could eventually lead to the extinction of his kind.

~*~*~

She saw the smirk and frowned more towards the random male. The guy was good looking, someone that she would not have a problem chatting up at a bar, but she would not have gone further than that. After all, her family could not know that she was in a bar at all, let alone talking to a random guy. What was odd was how the man seemed to sniff the air.

Miya raised a brow when the man laughed, he had a nice face when he laughed, but just because he was pretty didn't mean he could kill and kidnap people after all. She took a sip of the water before putting it back into her bag and slipping the pen into her back pocket. Now armed, she relaxed somewhat but kept on guard since this man had already proven to be very fast and strong. She would have to be vigilant if she was going to use the pen at a close range.

When the guy was done laughing and explained why he thought that she was chosen to be his mate, though it was confusing with all the words he used to describe it. When Micah said wife, however, it was Miya's turn to laugh. "Really? Wife? You really think that I would agree to be someone's wife after being kidnapped by that person. You're out of your mind" she stated once she was able to breathe again. Miya gave the other a look of derision. "I don't know how to break it to you, but I don't even know you. I don't even like you because, one, you see someone you like and you then go 'oh gee whiz I think I will just grab her and take her into the forest like some killer, golly nothing wrong with that,' two I think you are crazy and three you act like you aren't even human. You sniff at the air, you call me human like you aren't one, and you go on about this pull you feel for me. I would like to leave now thanks," she said, glaring as she slid over to the edge of the ledge and gripped the rocky side of the wall. Miya moved as quickly as she could to get the hell out of there and hopefully she would be able to get to the ground without much trouble. She started to slowly climb down, and remembered her one high school rock climbing class that she took. She kept her upper body close to the wall while letting her legs slowly lead the way.

Patru

Micah tilted his head to the side, trying hard not to start busting out laughing on the spot yet again. He wanted to keep a clear head since he had already revealed quite a bit of information to this girl. Since he did that, he couldn't let this human get back to her world without the fear of bringing death down onto his head and the clans. *'K, probably should have talked to father first.'* Micah thought to himself, dipping further into his thoughts to try and figure out how he was going to keep this girl under control.

Micah barely caught the woman crawling over the edge and slowly leaned over to watch the human attempt to climb down the near vertical cliff side. "You know if you make it down it won't be unscathed," he called to her with a smile on his face. It would take him less than three seconds to bound down the mountain and stand there waiting for her to reach the bottom. Micah decided to watch the girl for a little bit to see if she could actually get to the ground safely and if she couldn't, then Micah could be down there in seconds to catch her. Part of him was still debating though about letting the girl hit the ground; most likely breaking something in the process and then picking her up. It would be a good example to deter her from disobeying him again and start listening.

Miya stopped to breathe for a moment and raised her head up a bit to look at the guy. "I'm sure as hell going to try because I'm not going to wait around to be rescued by some over-pompous stuffed pinhead," she snapped in reply and then continued her slow climb down the rocky wall. She was trying hard to ignore the pain in her fingertips as well as the dull throb in her chest.

Every time she looked at that guy, something seemed to radiate through her. *'It doesn't matter if he is the hottest looking guy on earth, this is ridiculous,'* she told herself. Micah shook his head watching her slowly climb down the rocks; it was getting a bit tedious just watching her, so he decided that he should wait for her on the ground. Micah slipped over the edge to hang with one hand for a second before pushing against the wall and launching himself at the nearest treetop. He used the tree to slow his speed and jumped between two trees downwards, then landed safely on the ground in a crouching position. His breathing wasn't even heavy as he stood back to his full height. Micah slowly sauntered towards the base of the mountain and stared up at the girl, imagining the different scenarios that could play out if something happened to her on her climb down or that maybe he could do something to trip her up and force her to lose her grip.

Miya was still concentrating pretty hard on her climb; she didn't want to screw up and cause herself unnecessary pain or injury because that would probably just give the guy another excuse to keep her contained. "You might as well start looking for a ma-" she started to say as she took a brief second to look back up the cliff mid berating him only to find that the man was no longer standing on the ledge. *'Oh please don't be...'* she thought and carefully turned her head to look at the ground. *'Holy hell! How in the world did he get down there so fast?'* She thought and almost lost her footing. *'Well that's another tic in the not fully human box,'* she frowned in thought. "Look for your mate elsewhere because it's not me!" Miya screamed down to him, mostly because she was stalled out now. She was already too tired to try and climb back up the mountain but now he was down on the ground waiting for her.

Micah shook his head yet again, for being a human she was rather feisty - stupid, but feisty. "I hate to break it to you but it doesn't work that way," he called up to her and watched as she seemed to be looking sideways on both sides of her for something. He wasn't expecting her to try anything else, being in the position that she was in, but she surprised him.

Miya had quickly clawed at the mountain side and found a loose portion. She stabilized herself before pulling the rock from its nestled spot and chucked it down towards the guy's head. "Just leave me alone!" She called, hoping to distract him momentarily. Miya took the chance and released her grip to jump down the few feet she had to go to the ground. She felt a small twinge in her ankles from the impact with the ground, but she wasn't about to let that stop her. "Really, I'm just not that into you" she stated before turning and bolting away from him.

Micah was stunned at the woman's audacity to throw something at him, though even more so when she made it to the ground unharmed. He had even been nice enough to try and introduce himself as well as fix his tiny screw up, and yet this girl was challenging him by throwing things at him and then running. *'Well guess I'll just have to teach her a different lesson',* he thought to himself, and turned to catch up with his mate.

He was only jogging at a light pace but he was already gaining on her. She was fast for a human, but not fast enough. *'Time to have some fun',* he thought to himself, and sprinted towards a tree, using it to launch himself over the girl. He landed gracefully in front of her now in his full wolf form. He was already breaking several rules already, so what would a few more matter? Micah straightened his back on all four paws, putting him well over the woman's height. In human form he was already towering over her, but in wolf form he was slightly taller. Micah raised his hackles, baring his teeth a bit and emitted a low territorial growl. This was the last thing he would attempt to get the human to understand that she didn't stand a chance against him. If that didn't get the girl to comply even a little, then Micah would have no choice but to drag her back to the village.

"Well you're just going to have to figure something else out because I want nothing to do with you and I don't want to be your mate, end of story" Miya screamed over her shoulder as she weaved through trees hoping to gain more distance between them. She could feel her body losing the will to keep going but her mind was overwriting any exhaustion that she felt at the moment. She wasn't one for the sport of running or track, Miya was more the swimming and biking kind of person. It had been a few minutes since she heard any sound from the man which got her hopes up that he was finally going to give up on her.

Boy was she wrong.

She skidded to a stop as she saw the man fly over her and land not too far away. She was frozen stiff that in the place of the man she had been used to seeing there now was a beautiful and deadly looking white wolf. Miya's fear spiked higher just at the sight of the beast and her brain finally snapped together all the strange facts in the last couple of hours. "Fucking hell!" She shivered when the wolf growled, those silver eyes glaring at her so intently and keeping her trapped.

Micah could almost taste the fear that now hung in the air and his attempts at reasoning with the woman were gone. He gave another soft growl in warning, but he watched as she finally turned back around and ran. Micah dropped his head to the ground watching her run again. This time the thrill of the chase sang through his veins. He lifted his head to the sky, parting his jowls and letting his voice carry among the trees in the wind. This human would now be subject to the hunt.

Cinci

Micah got a responding howl from some nearby pack mates, and his plan started to formulate. Micah launched himself forward, his massive paws digging into the ground and pushing him forward each time they hit the ground.

Miya gulped down air almost as fast as it left her lungs. *'What the fuck am I going to do?!'* She thought as she heard more howls, joining the first one. She glanced around mid-step trying to see if they were near her – yet. *'The pen,'* she remembered, the small weapon in her back pocket might not do a lot to protect her, but it could buy her enough time to get further away. Miya wanted to look over her shoulder badly, but from her vast array of watching horror films she had kept in mind that people who look back usually end up tripping and dying quickly, so she kept her eyes focused forward. Another ear-shattering howl erupted behind her, as if the white wolf was irritated that the others weren't there yet. Miya took that moment to turn sharply, using the trunk of a tree to keep up her speed as well as the path, and ran head long straight for the wolf. It was a tactic that she saw working out in her head, but she wasn't so sure it would work in real life, but she had to try something. Anything to get the wolf to halt his pursuit, even for a minute.

Her plan couldn't have worked out more perfectly, her stunt of running at the wolf had him skidding to a stop and Miya took that chance. She made a small jump and allowed herself to hit the ground sideways; sliding along the forest floor with the momentum she had gained. She pulled the pen from her back pocket as she came near the wolf and plunged the writing utensil into the wolf's shoulder and dragged it from the back of his shoulder to the guy's front pec while sliding underneath the oversized wolf. She could feel some blood dripping down onto her face but she didn't care at the moment, all she could think was run, get away and do whatever it took. Once she was clear from under the wolf and a good distance behind him, she jumped to her feet and pushed off the ground to continue running south, back the way they had come when she climbed off the mountain ledge and hopefully out of the forest. She didn't care so long as she could find a road or something, then he would call for help.

Miya kept up a serpentine pattern while running through the trees. She still had no idea how many more wolves there were or how close they were. Unfortunately, her stamina was running out and it wouldn't be long before she knew that the wolves would be on her. She stopped, huffing and puffing while looking around to see if there was a good tree she could climb. After all, she really would rather not go with the man now. Miya could just see it now, meeting the in-laws. The guy's family would eat her alive, her own family probably disowning her and saying they never had a daughter just to save themselves. Her steps faltered at her passive thoughts. 'Right, let's keep the mind on running', her golden brown orbs refocusing on the path in front of her. Miya's long black hair clung to the side of her face as well as her sweat-soaked black and white t-shirt. She was a sitting duck just standing there, the prominent browns and greens of the forest made her stick out easily where she was.

Shortly after Micah hunched forward from the wound his mate inflicted on him, two more smaller rust colored wolves flanked him, and helped him back onto his paws.

'What's going on Mic?' The wolf on his right whined.

'Why'd you call us like this?' Came a yelp from the wolf on his left.

'It's time that I stopped running from being Alpha', Micah barked

out and ended in a predatory growl.

'What are you talking about?' They both questioned.

'That human up ahead is mine. Box her in', Micah ordered.

The two rust-colored wolves shifted their attention in time to see the human weaving to avoid trees. They weren't sure exactly what was going on right now, but unable to ignore the command of a higher-ranking wolf, they both took off. Splitting apart just up ahead to circle around and block the human's path while Micah came from behind.

Miya glanced back briefly; color draining from her face and two more wolves came barreling towards her. She quickly chose the tallest tree she could find and, as quickly as she could, scaled the trunk of the tree to the highest, thickest branch her body could get to. Her backpack felt heavy on her back but she wasn't about to let go of it. She may need something in it, like another weapon, since she left the first one in the white wolf after stabbing him. After finding a moment to relax and breathe, she could feel a burning sensation growing over her leg, assuming she had gotten hurt from sliding under the wolf and across the rocks in the dirt. Miya made a note to check later to make sure she didn't hurt herself more, but at the moment she was trying to block out the pain so she could focus on the threats that circled below her now.

Micah ran headlong, his eyes glazing over with the intent of capturing his mate once again. The pain that radiated from his shoulder was nothing compared to what he had experienced in his younger days, so it was easy enough to ignore. *'She will not get away. Call my father and the hunters',* Micah barked the order at the two after catching up to the others at the base of a tree, his ears perked high on his head and then dropped as he lifted his head once more. His howl reached up towards the sky, mixing with the pain that ran through him and driving him harder to capture his mate once more. His howl was joined by a higher pitched one coming from both rust-colored wolves. The message had been sent and the howling died off. Micah was pacing about the base of the tree while the other two stared at him curiously.

'Explain before...' one started

'Your father gets here.' The other finished.

Micah briefly turned his head to look at both of them before returning his gaze up into the tree branches, not saying a word.

~*~*~

'What the hell is going on?!'

Now that voice was unmistakable and even sent a slight shiver down Micah's spine. However, the other two wolves' ears fell flat against their skull and seemed to shrink away.

'You smell that human?' Micah questioned his father, hoping to keep the man's attention off of him for at least the time being.

'Of course I do. What is she doing in our territory?' His father's voice bellowed throughout the thoughts of the pack members.

'She's important and cannot be allowed to get away' Micah told his father, dancing around the real reason he didn't want the guy to get away.

His father started barking out orders to the six wolves that were with him, trusting his son, and while Micah and his small group kept circling around the tree with the human in it.

Miya could hear more of them coming and more howls, her fear taking full effect. She looked for any sign of hope; her cell phone was still in her bag but she wasn't sure how much battery life it had. She rested her forehead against the tree and felt the blood of her so-called 'mate' dripping down her cheek and temple while mixing with her sweat. Miya took a few long deep breaths to slow her heart rate before she hyperventilated and then pulled her backpack to rest in front of her. She quickly dug into her bag, frustrated that she hadn't kept her phone in her back pocket like she usually did, but she finally felt the familiar slick plastic case against her hand. Miya was excited, maybe her luck was turning around and she pulled the phone up to eye level and her hopes were dashed. She had two percent battery life, *'Fuck me. That's not gonna cut it,'* she groaned in her head, she was as good as dead. Miya hung her head, feeling the defeat; her eyes cleared a little to see ten wolves now at the base of the tree. She reeled back, a breath catching in her throat. *'Think, think, think,'* she thought to herself, and then rummaged through her bag again. There were a few thick medical textbooks she could throw at them if any should try to climb the tree after her, to buy some time, hopefully.

Sase

Micah made another round around the tree, avoiding his father's gaze for a little bit more, but as he came back to the north side of the tree where his father was, he couldn't help but stop in his tracks. His father's glare could be just as bad as his bite at times. If things were to end right here, then his father would surely start bombarding him with questions. Micah could feel the blood flowing from his open wound on his shoulder but for some reason his back leg throbbed like he had been bulldozed by a rock.

'You better quickly give me one good reason as to why there is a human in our territory,' his father growled at him, and Micah saw the hair on his father's hunches raise. Even for him, that was a scary sight. Micah may have been one of the largest male wolves in his pack, some said even more so when his father was his age, but that still didn't change the fact that his father had more muscle on him.

Micah looked at his father and then around the area once more, refusing to answer his father.

'Got her.' One of the rust-colored wolves whined loudly and everyone but Micah's father looked up.

However, Micah was too distracted now trying to come up with a plan to get the girl out of the tree without causing too much harm to the other. Unfortunately, his father had other ideas at the moment.

Staring up into the tree and walking in circles, Micah was pacing until he felt a tank slam into his side. It took a few seconds for him to realize what had happened and he bounced back to his paws.

__'Don't just stand there all of you. Get that human out of the tree by any means necessary. I'll deal with my son'__, his father barked and charged Micah again. The speed at which the two bounced off of each other looked painful. His father's almost pitch black fur seemed to meld with his silver-shining snow-white fur as they collided over and over again. He knew that his father would keep at this until he gave a good reason for what was going on, but he just couldn't bring himself to blurt out that the human in the tree was his mate.

Two of the wolves shifted back to human form, trying to avoid being run over by the oversized wolves fighting, and turned to the tree. "This can only successfully end one way...meaning if you listen to us, then you won't die. However, if the Alpha orders your death in order to keep the pack safe because you refused to listen, then it's over for you," one of the men called up the tree, hoping to get at least a decent response from the human.

Miya watched as the wolves seemed to talk among themselves, making her golden eyes look around for whatever was going on. She had enough power for one call so she turned off her phone to save it until she knew where she was. Miya saw Micah turning in circles, but the throbbing in her leg took her mind off the wolves for a minute so she could look over her leg. Miya sighed with relief when nothing seemed to be broken but just bruised really badly.

She watched, stunned, as one of the rusted fur wolves whined something and a bunch of the wolves moved closer to the tree. Miya gripped tightly to the branch she was seated on, she was much too high for them to make a grab for her at the moment and thankful she could knock them down with her books before they could reach her. She hated the idea of using her books like that, but if it saved her life, it was worth it.

Miya internally freaked as the big black wolf attacked the white one, and winced each time they hit against each other. She hoped the guy was getting punished for kidnapping her. 'Serves him right,' she thought to herself while watching the whole ordeal. "Werewolf or not, any sane person should know to take a person to dinner first before jumping them...maybe...' her thoughts trailed, watching the spectacle until a voice called out to her, hearing words that reminded her of the guy who dragged her into this forest.

"Oh yeah, you know what - you are just as good at talking to victims as the last guy. Though I think the white one gets the gold, I hope you don't mind second place," she said, glaring down at the wolves. Miya was not going to come down no matter what, but that didn't mean she couldn't talk. "Look, I just want to go home and forget any of this happened, just keep that white wolf away from me and we are all just peachy" she said pointing to the two fighting wolves, "and if anyone tries to climb up here I am going to hit them in the head with some very hefty medical books!" She stated while glaring down at the now human wolves.

No plan was working out, the two that stood there trying to figure out ways to convince her to come down nor the Alpha and his son. Blood had splattered the forest floor from the many bites Alpha and Micah had gotten on each other while the others continued to circle the tree trying to come up with something.

"You do realize that the white wolf is the Alpha's son," one called up to her as the other circled around the tree to start judging the branches and paths he could take.
"Not to mention even if you hit us with those books it will hurt, slow us down a bit, but I'm sure you don't have enough books to get all of us," the one that had been circling the tree had finally called up to her.
The other guy started laughing as well, the situation started to get to him as funny.
"Besides, your aim from there is crap," the first guy called once

again.

Two other wolves shifted back into human form to help out while the other four stayed in their fur as back up if they got the girl out of the tree.

'I'll explain later, father...' Micah barked out just as his father slammed into him and forced his body to collide with a nearby tree. *'...it's a bit complicated.'* He finished when he was able to get back to his paws. His father didn't let up though, and pounced on him again, snapping his jowls around Micah's throat, forcing him to submit. Micah whined out his surrender and his father released him.

Both of them backed away from each other and shifted to human form. **"Explain now, why there is a human in my territory that needs to be contained,"** his father snapped at him.

Micah picked himself up off the ground, blood dripping from an open wound on his forehead while there were others that mirrored on his arms, down his legs and across his back. Without saying a word to his father, Micah looked up into the tree. "Would you like to tell my father why you are here? It might be better on your part if he hears it from you. That way he won't see you as the wimpy human he thinks you are right now." Micah called up to her while taking shallow breaths because his ribs hurt too much at the moment. "Seeing how you were able to wound me. And that's quite a feat, but I'm sure your shoulder can't be feeling too well after that either." Micah shouted once again with a smile on his face. Just another reason for him to believe this human was his mate. He knew that before his father's beating that he hadn't injured his legs, which meant the human must have.

Miya grimaced as pain started to bloom all over her body. She hadn't hurt herself that badly running or climbing the tree, so why would pain be blossoming in her body? She rubbed her shoulder, and looked down at everyone standing at the base of the tree.

"What? The guy kidnapped me right off of campus!" She yelled down before turning a stern look to the man calling out to her. She was getting a bit sick of one of the wolves that was laughing, remembering earlier that this one had questioned her aim. She pulled out the thickest book she had in her bag and lined up her shot with the guy's head. She took a short breath before chucking the book; she watched it soar down quickly to the unsuspecting target and nailing the guy right in the head. Miya smirked even if he felt like the pain was intensifying. "You were saying earlier, chuckles?" She called down, a laugh of her own coming out. She had thrown her pathophysiology book. That damn thing had always given her back problems with how thick it was.

After the two fighting wolves change back into human forms, Miya was shocked that questions and demands started flying around. The order of why a human was here in their territory towards the alpha's son had Miya grinning. 'Ooh sonny boy is going to get into trouble.' She thought and just hoped to live to see the end of it. She rubbed her forehead lightly, it felt like a small head pain, but why was it acting up now? When Micah called up for her to explain what happened, her blood boiling more. "Are you fucking kidding me right now? You came up to me on campus, picked me up and threw me over your shoulder like a caveman and brought me in here. Talking about a pull and mates. Here's a news flash, I am not your mate!" She yelled down, shaking a fist at the man before moving to grip her shoulder. The pain around her body felt muted like it wasn't her pain or some sort of growth pain.

"I just want to go home, get a warm bath and relax to get rid of my pain, so just leave me alone!" She yelled at everyone "and I want my book back!" she added as an afterthought.

Textbooks weren't cheap.

Sapte

"Dumbass," the other wolf from earlier called to his buddy who had the book land on his head and was now lying flat on the ground.

"I heard that," the guy called back, even though he was laughing at what had just happened. He had a nice blooming pain in his skull and was seeing stars right now, but he was thankful that it was only a book and not a back of bricks. "So, Imma just gonna lay here for the moment," he announced, and the Alpha waved him off.

As the human started yelling out her frustration that Micah had kidnapped her and claimed they were mates, Micah's father turned to him. **"She's your mate!"** He exclaimed, his anger spiking once more and causing two of the pack mates to jump in front of the alpha so he wouldn't kill Micah. **"You better hope to god that this is some sick joke that you end now,"** his father growled to him. Micah could see his father start to change, but still being in the early stages, he hoped that his father would listen to reason.

"I'm not fond of the idea either and I was hoping to have more time with the girl to figure it out but she went ballistic on me and sliced my shoulder with some kind of pen." Micah held his hands up in front of his chest, hoping to get his father to see that he was not doing this on purpose.

"Prove it!" His father ordered.

Micah's eyes darted about the area trying to think of some way to show his father that he was being serious and didn't just screw up by revealing their secret to a human, nor the fact that it was his choice that his mate was a human. "I hope you are good at withstanding pain, human." Micah called up to her.

He raised his left hand, allowing his nails to lengthen and sliced his uninjured shoulder open about three inches. It would only take about a day and a really large meal for all his wounds to heal but Micah was used to the pain. Humans, on the other hand, had no idea what real pain was, especially pain in the eyes of werewolves. As Micah's claws broke free of his shoulder, all eyes turned towards the human and were waiting to see the outcome, especially his father.

While the alpha and his son were having their bickering match, Miya was snickering softly to herself while looking at the two who were talking to her. *'These two are funny,'* she thought, but it was too bad that they wanted her to come down for all the wrong reasons. "If I come out of this alive I will buy you a drink," she called down to the guy she had beaned in the head with her book and couldn't help the large grin plastered across her face. After all, she enjoyed good company and the two clowns seemed like they would be good for a laugh.

Once again, the testosterone-filled idiots couldn't keep their rage in check and the outburst from the alpha made her jump this time. It looked like the alpha was angrier at his son than anything else, which was odd to her. It seemed that the outburst even warranted the others present to jump in between the two to keep them from fighting once again or for the son to get hurt. "I went ballistic?! You fucking kidnapped me and told me I didn't have a choice in the matter!" She screamed, thinking about aiming a book at the fucker, but he was hurt enough and she never would willingly hurt someone to the point of bleeding unless needed.

Her thoughts didn't progress further than that because she was curious as to why the guy called to her about the need to handle pain. *'Why do I need to withstand pain? It's not like anyone is climbing the tree to get me,'* she thought to herself, because she felt pretty safe for the moment...she hoped.

Miya looked around and her eyes landed on the father briefly before she saw the guy lengthen his nails. Her eyes widened to the size of dinner plates when her kidnapper started to rip into his own shoulder. What Miya didn't expect was an excruciating pain to erupt in her shoulder in time with Micah ripping into his shoulder. Her hand shot to her shoulder, gripping it tightly as a hiss of pain escaped her clenched teeth. When all eyes were on her, she was bewildered, but she had a feeling that it had something to do with the pain she was now feeling. After all, why else would the guy warn her ahead of time after the alpha snapped at his son to prove it. "F-fuck" she hissed, moving to lean her head against the trunk of the tree again. Miya pulled the shoulder of her shirt down enough to see what the hell was digging into her shoulder but found nothing, the skin wasn't even broken. So why was her shoulder hurting?

Everyone was stunned except Micah. Micah had already felt in his heart that this was his mate and he hated to cause the girl pain like that, but there was no other way or time right now to show his father that he wasn't lying. Micah watched his father as he continued to stare up at the girl, as if his father was trying to will a different reaction from the female in the tree. He watched as Alpha took a deep breath, exhaling angrily and turning to Micah, **"This will do for now, but this is not over and as for the rest of you...this does not spread to the others until I know what to do"**. Alpha commanded and everyone nodded their heads besides Micah, who stood there staring up at his mate while clutching his freshly wounded shoulder and seeing the same action on the human.

Micah still wasn't too fond of the idea of having a human mate, so long as she would give him pups. But to have a human mate in a pack of wolves would force Micah to be extra careful and extra protective, just in case any of the others, mostly the females in his village, got it in their heads to try and eliminate his mate, since the human would be an easy target for them.

"I would like to address you by your name, human. If you are willing to give it to me. If not, then I have no choice but to either call you human or Micah's mate. To be respectful, you may call me Alpha for now. If things prove to be as my son has spoken, then you will have the privilege to learn my name," Micah heard his father announce up towards his mate, in a tone that his father only reserved for women of high standards. At least his father was actually being nice to his mate and not pretending just to get her out of the tree and then kill her. The other wolves with them were even a bit stunned by the tone the Alpha was using.

"Second off, I would like to personally apologize for my son's primitive behavior. I promise you that he was raised better than that. Lastly, if you will be so kind as to come down now, I will guarantee that you will not be harmed," his father continued, making Micah start to pace. He wanted his mate out of the tree and hoped that word would not spread through the pack about who his mate was until he could come to terms with it himself.

Opt

Miya frowned at how high and mighty the older man's tone was but at the moment this guy seemed to be the one she should keep on his good side. Though she didn't like how she had to give up her name yet this man got to hold back his, she didn't really understand the dynamics of werewolves. "The names Miya, and that's all you're getting. I would say nice to meet you but I think it would have been better under different circumstances," she called down.

If she had known that the man was addressing her like he did the high ranking woman of his pack then she probably would have been nicer in her words. She did like though that Alpha had said that his son was raised better than acting like a caveman, and Miya had hoped to see the man's mother slap him around a little for the way that she had been treated.

When she was given a guarantee that she would be safe, she tentatively decided that it was time to get out of the tree. That and her ass was starting to hurt from straddling the tree branch. "Alright, but I would like to have my space, my shoulder and ribs hurt like hell," she said rubbing at her side a bit, the pain in her legs from earlier had subsided the moment the pain in her shoulder started. Miya secured everything inside her bag before slipping her arms back through the straps and double checking that her cellphone was hidden in a pocket of her jeans. Slowly she moved down the tree, making sure that her footing was secure before moving because all she needed right now was to fall out of the tree breaking something and be taken care of by these brutes. When she got closer to the base of the tree she hesitated for a moment until all of them backed up like the alpha promised and then she hopped the rest of the way down onto the grass. Miya brushed her clothes back into place then turned and gave them all looks to warn them again to stay away from her. She retrieved her book from her earlier throw and turned to the Alpha. "I don't like being told what I can or can't do," she announced, turning a condescending smile towards her kidnapper and finally replaced her book in her bag. "I would like to go home now. I have a lot of work to do and classes tomorrow." Miya stated simply.

She looked Alpha over since she was able to get a better look at him from the ground and then looked to Micah. "I can also take a look at your shoulder. I have a first aid kit in my bag and those wounds look like they need to be treated soon." She said not in an unkind way but borderline stiffness like she had to say it because she was going to be in the medical field.

Alpha nodded his head with a bit of a smile, the girl had guts to talk to him like that but let it go with the thought that the human didn't know any better. They all watched as Miya climbed down from the tree, and as promised everyone took several steps away from the human. An unspoken order from the Alpha echoing through their mental link. Alpha stayed where he was however since it was his right as head of the pack but his eyes did drift over to his son who looked like he wanted to pounce on Miya.

"Vin, Matt! Restrain Micah!" Alpha ordered.

"You've got to be fu-" Micah started to hiss when the two bolted at him and locked their arms around him. Vin restrained one arm with his own as Matt wrapped an arm around Micha's neck. Micah choked a bit at the force that was used but knew that if he truly didn't mind screwing up his body more then he would have fought back more, but his mind reminded him that if he did that then Miya would hurt more.

Once Alpha was content that his son had calmed down he turned back to the human. **"I am sorry to say that the reaction you had and the pain you are experiencing is in fact due to you being my son's mate and thus you will have to come with us until this situation can be resolved"** Alpha placed a hand on the girl's shoulder, making sure she stayed where she was and to show that he actually did feel sympathy for the situation she was in. A low possessive growl emitted from Micah when he saw his father touching Miya, only to be returned with a glared and silent order that had him lowering his head ever so slightly.

"You will be able to look over his wounds and your own when we get back to the village..." Alpha explained and turned his head towards a granite-colored wolf. **"Derek, run ahead and make sure our arrival goes as planned. I'll escort Miya and my son through the back path while the others will take the main route"** Alpha ordered and Derek barked his understanding before taking off.

"Now that everything is in motion, shall we get moving?" Alpha turned his eyes back to Miya with a soft expression on his face. Miya nodded her agreement, knowing that running right now would be futile since there were so many others present. She noted how Alpha stayed where he was while the others seemed to bow to him.

'I guess they share a lot with real wolves' Miya thought to herself as she studied the way everyone around her moved and acted. She glanced behind at Micah, restrained by the other two, still a bit stunned at the treatment and wondered if it was necessary until she saw the hungry look in the man's eyes, that was when she was more than thankful for the others restraining him.

She could feel a sort of tightness around her own neck, and that still puzzled her and her curiosity wanted to be quenched. When she looked back at Alpha she realized that the man was much taller than she had first noticed. *'Dammit, why are they all so tall? Is it a werewolf thing?'* She quarried in her head as they started to move. "I would like to point out once again that I am not his mate. I don't even know him," she said, not trying to be disrespectful, after all she knew how to talk to father's with honor issues.

Miya turned to look at Micah when another growl came from him. She wanted to fish for more information, she had to understand: why her? How does this happen? Is it random?

Miya looked at the hand on her shoulder when Alpha didn't remove it once they started walking and debated about smacking it away but thought better of that action because the grip alone felt stronger then she'd be able to handle. She was getting tired of people touching her without her consent.

Miya's heart almost rejoiced when she heard that this could be resolved. 'Thank god,' she screamed in her head. Hopefully she could go home soon once she could explain that she felt no pull towards pretty boy.

Nouă

"If I may, I'd like to ask about your son's behavior and a few things he said. I was unable to get much out of him and I am hoping that you will be willing to answer them," she stated diplomatically, her golden orbs keeping a close watch on Micah from the corner of her eye. She still didn't trust that the two holding Micah would keep him that way and she wanted to get as much information as she could. This was probably a once in a lifetime chance even though it came about in a very heart-thumping way, but the father seemed nice enough, if not more willing to answer questions, she hoped. "The first question would be as to why your son felt the need to kidnap me, instead of just buying me a drink or something first? Another is, he said I didn't have a choice in the matter from this point on and I would like to know if he had planned on keeping me in the forest when I have a life I need to get back to?"

Alpha shook his head briefly at the girl, trying not to let her ignorance of the matter at hand get to him. Even the proof earlier was enough for him, that his son and this human were connected. Alpha had to keep reminding himself that the human race didn't see or believe in anything they didn't want to and did not teach their offspring about the Loup Garou anymore. Alpha looked over his shoulder, making sure that Micah was behaving himself despite being restrained with his mate mere feet in front of him.

"Look here Miya, you have to understand that our culture is different from yours in a few ways. I'm sure you have already grasped that we are not human, we are known as Loup

Garou, but to your people we are more commonly referred to as shape shifters or werewolves. However, nothing like what your movies or books portray us as," Alpha began explaining, since they had a bit of a walk back to the village from where they were at. "To answer your first question, in all honesty, my son probably panicked when he felt drawn to you. It's something that happens to our kind. It's like a giant sign flashing to let the wolf know that he or she has found the one for them. The reason for his panic is because my son is going to be the next Alpha soon and, as my rule, he had to find his mate before I would willingly step down and let him take over. With that said, no Alpha in many generations has ever had a human mate, they have all been of our species and I'm not so sure I want to disrupt that tradition, even now." Alpha continued to explain and finally dropped his hand from Miya's shoulder, feeling that he could trust that the girl wouldn't run off. "It is tradition that Micah's mate would live with him in our village but that normally wouldn't be a big deal because his mate should have been one of our kind. Having a human as a mate is...not our forte and thus I am apprehensive about letting this continue. However, I can't exactly forbid my son from tracking you down and being with you. That would be like me telling my wife and mate that I would rather kill her than be with her. Are you starting to understand?" Alpha hoped that the human was starting to grasp the severity of the situation and would at least cooperate, because even if he didn't like that his son's mate was a human, he could never make Micah choose between his mate and the pack. Alpha already knew what the choice would be. Alpha, though, was not going to hesitate to suggest that his son take a Loup Garou bride as well, for the sake of the pack and that he could keep his human mate in the human world.

Miya eyed Alpha when he started explaining the answers to her questions and she was trying to take in as much information as she could. "It was rather easy to notice slight irregularities that most humans do not exhibit as normal behavior. What with your son sniffing the air and talking of 'you humans.' Not very good at hiding," she said as she bobbed her head side to side. Miya gave a sharp nod when Alpha said that she probably thought of them as werewolves. When Alpha said that his son probably panicked when he saw him and did what he did, Miya's brows knitted together, *'what an odd thing to do when panicking,'* she thought. "So because I'm human, he thought that kidnapping me in the middle of campus was the best idea?" She asked, trying not to let a laugh escape because the whole idea was just absurd. Miya could understand the pressure of wanting a mate of their own kind. She guessed it would be like making sure the line continued on and there would be another alpha to protect a pack much like wolves in nature. "So I feel his pain and he can feel mine? In your world is this called being mated? Does that mean the mates are meant to fall for each other? Do you know if it is something in your DNA?" She started to ramble, something she did when she was overwhelmed and falling back on the knowledge that she had – her human knowledge that was. She was trying to figure out what connected all of what they were saying to what humans had come to know through science and modern medicine.

"I think I understand. In your species, it is normal for each wolf to have a 'fated' mate. I think that evolution helped with that to make sure that your kind would not die out, and in this 'bond' both parties would feel attraction, possessiveness and other feelings to insure offspring. Seeing how your son is next in line to be the alpha, a position he was born for by this breeding process, I can understand why you would be reluctant to let him go after me. Though is there that much of a difference between your DNA and that of a human that having a human mate wouldn't be good? Would the mating still produce offspring?" Miya questioned more, her mind was starting to become jumbled and she only realized after asking that it sounded like she was going along with all of this – with being Micah's mate but she wasn't. She was just the curious sort. "Not to mention you said that you are apprehensive; does that mean you have a way to break that bond?" She asked once, her brain had become too tangled to think of anything else.

Alpha's brows knitted together, this girl sure could talk a lot, but it seemed as though she was grasping most of everything that he was saying. **"You seem to have the jest of it. But I'm sorry to inform you that I don't even know why it happens like this and we don't question it either. So long as my pack can survive, then I am fine with it,"** Alpha explained to Miya and then led her to the left of the main path. The village wasn't too much further ahead and soon their conversation would come to an end. **"My son wasn't lying when he said that you didn't have a choice, and neither does my son. You are his mate from here on out. What I was referring to would be that if things work out, you will be able to return to your human life on the agreement that you can be trusted with our secret, but that Micah would still be able to be with you and spend his time with you. However, with that said if he truly wishes to become Alpha of the pack I would require him to take a female bride of our species,"** Alpha explained.

Micah started growling and shifting within the grasp of the other two at his father's words. He was making it rather difficult for them to hold him. "I will do no such fucking thing! Miya is my mate; I refuse to take any others as such, even if it is just a ruse," Micah spit out.

He swung a leg out catching Matt's legs and tripping him up, but unfortunately, Vin's hold on his neck tightened. "If you make me take a Loup Garou bride and have her bear my pups, then I swear to the moon I will kill her and the pups!" Micah growled even though he started coughing from the extra force Vin was placing around his neck until Matt was able to get his grip back on him. "Miya is my one and only mate, I refuse to let anyone else bear my pups!" Micah growled out as a final matter of fact statement. Alpha halted the trek into the village, turning sharply to stalk up to his son and pulling his face up so they were looking into each other's eyes. **"If I command it, it will be obeyed. As my son, you of all people should know that better than anyone,"** Alpha's voice boomed before releasing his grip on Micah's chin.

Zece

The pack members that were with them coward at Alpha's tone, even Miya shrunk a little, but what surprised her most was Micah still continued to growl and fight. Miya's heart fluttered when Micah said he would not have any other mate but her. She felt all the pressure that was being placed on Micah's body to keep him contained. Miya's hand moved to lightly touch her own throat, feeling the pressure build and her heart started to flip out.

Her heart all but stopped when the guy started screaming about pups, *'pups are children,'* she reminded herself, and when she could breathe Miya worked up her courage and stared directly into Micah's eyes. "I hate to burst your bubble, but I don't plan on having children anytime soon...if ever. Not that I could probably have children with you, since our DNA is different." She flat out told him and didn't wait to hear any stupid retort the guy had before turning back to Alpha.

"Will it not seem odd that a human will be in your camp? And that you have your son being handled like such?" She bluntly asked, after all she felt it was her duty to say something about the way the guy was being handled, even if she didn't feel any sort of romantic notion towards him. Miya didn't want the guy getting hurt worse because the pain she was experiencing was bad, so she assumed he felt worse.

Alpha had slowed their pace into the village to give his son time to calm down. He didn't need his son passing out from lack of oxygen or Miya being hurt in the process. That wouldn't look good for them if this human got scared again. **"This will not be the first time my son has been treated like this, so please do not worry about that. Also, his body can sustain more damage than this before he is in true danger."** Alpha explained, hoping to quell any fear the girl might have.

Miya blinked when Alpha said this was not the first time his son had been treated this way. *'Good lord, what has he done for this to be a normal thing?'* She thought, but nodded her head in acknowledgement.

"Damn straight I can take more than this and pups will be had!" Micah screamed before Alpha motioned for Matt to cover Micah's mouth.

Matt was a bit hesitant since his buddy could be pretty hot-headed when he was like this. Matt was afraid of being bitten by Micah. With a warning snarl from Alpha, Matt finally covered Micah's mouth as tightly as he could while still helping Vin to maintain control.

Once satisfied that he wouldn't be interrupted again, Alpha turned his sights back to Miya. **"Whether you are male or female Loup Garou - if the right measures are taken, then either gender can bear the next generation and I'm sure that the formula could be tweaked for a human as well, but as I have stated before - no Alpha in our pack has had a human mate. So I am inclined to agree with you on the fact that you will not be baring the next generation."** Alpha was finally able to state, awarding a very possessive growl from Micah. **"As for now, I have chosen this path of having you come into the village for a reason. My home, as well as Micah's right now, is there..."** Alpha pointed to the back porch of a three-story hand-built house, resembling a modern day log cabin and not giving Miya the chance to question this process of male's being able to have offspring, not to mention making it possible for a human to bear pups.

"Take Micah to the basement, and use the appropriate measures." Alpha ordered Vin and Matt just as they reached the back door of the home. Both jerked their heads, showing they understood and quickly pulled Micah into the house, and making sure that he wasn't going to try anything stupid, while Alpha led Miya into the house and towards the kitchen.

"Please tell me there was some kind of mix up?" A female voice traveled to them, her tone shocked and slightly hopeful.

Alpha turned to see his wife, who was walking up to them, and he sighed lightly, **"I'm afraid that this is no joke, but before we get to that. Honey, this is Miya, Micah's mate. Miya, this is my wife."** Alpha introduced them and his wife walked up to her.

She looked Miya over, sniffing the air slightly like Micah had done, but her face seemed to soften almost instantly. "You are a lovely young lady, Miya. You can just call me Alora. Unlike my stiff husband and apparently rude son, you can be yourself around me. I won't bite your head off and please excuse my shock from earlier. I am happy for you and my son, really. It's just...I wasn't expecting this but be it as it may, please make yourself at home. What's ours is yours as well" she told Miya in a sweet, almost bell-like tone now. "Can I get you anything to drink? Or eat? I'm sure you are starving" she perkily asked, and moved back into the kitchen.

Miya was at a loss for words, everything was happening so quickly. One minute Alpha was explaining information that she so desperately wanted, the next he was ordering his son to be taken to a basement and then bewilderment crossed her face when Alpha's wife hurried up to them. She quietly looked around, ignoring Alora's question for now. Miya followed Alpha and Alora into the kitchen. "It's a pleasure to meet you, Alora, and might I say you have a lovely name," she finally said, when they were in the kitchen. "I don't really want to rain on the parade, but I don't intend to stay nor use your home as I like but I appreciate the invitation. As Alpha said, my name is Miya and

I have to say, I was not expecting this today after my classes as well," she said, nodding to Alora when she said that she could make herself at home. "Some water would be nice and I really should see to tending to your son's shoulder wound, I'm afraid I'm the reason he has it," Miya admitted to Alpha and his wife. At the end of the day, she didn't want to be the cause of someone getting an infection that could cost the guy to lose his arm. She could still feel the pain from the wounds all over her body.

Alora tilted her head, this human was strange but she had seen worse before her husband found her. She smiled at Miya, thankful that her husband could get the human here and in one piece no less. Alora nodded her head at the request for water and promptly retrieved it for the young woman. "Micah will be fine for a little bit, you look like you could use a nice hot shower and maybe some pain killers." Alora said after Miya finished off half the glass of water and then gently pushed her to a set of stairs that lead up to the second floor. "The bathroom's the second door on your right; there are fresh towels in the cupboard in the hallway. After that you can go and see Micah," she told Miya, and made sure that she would listen to her.

Alora could be the sweetest and nicest person you could ever meet, but cross her and she would become your worst nightmare. When she was sure that the girl was out of ear shot, Alora turned to her husband. "Alright, why don't you start explaining from the beginning about what the hell is going on and why my son is bloodied and chained in the basement like when he first started training" Alora's voice pulled almost a 180 degree turn.

Alpha, on the other hand, was used to it. He loved it when his wife was feisty, but right now was a highly sensitive situation. **"Alright, but until Micah calms down I won't be able to get both sides of the story or all the facts. However, I will do my best. Are you gonna start on the preparations for tonight's feast?"** Alpha started off and then watched as Alora bobbed her head up and down.

"Just give me everything you know so I can be prepared and, of course, dear. Things are going as smoothly as ever." While Alora moved about the kitchen, Alpha began relaying everything that he knew and what he had concluded so far, as well as some of his solutions to the predicament of Miya and their son.

Unsprezece

Miya was surprised that she was ushered off so quickly and with an odd offer. Taking a shower in the home of her kidnappers seemed silly, but she wondered if the reason she was pushed up the stairs was because Alora wanted to talk to her husband alone.

With a shrug of her shoulders she ascended the stairs and glanced about the hallway, wondering how many rooms were on this floor. She briefly wondered if Micah's room was here somewhere but quickly shook the thought from her head and promptly headed to the door where Alora said the bathroom was at. As much as Miya would have loved to snoop around, it probably wouldn't be the greatest idea because she was sure that, Loup Garou, she remembered they were called, would smell where she had been. She was not about to chance her survival by quenching her curiosity.

Inside the bathroom, Miya was able to breathe a little better, she wasn't being watched like a hawk or contained by grabbing hands. She began looking around the bathroom, finding that it was a nice large room with everything neatly in place and easy to find what was needed.

Miya finally removed her bag from her shoulders and placed it on the toilet seat. She cautiously stripped from her clothes after finding a towel for when she was done. She gently laid her clothes over her bag and turned her attention to the shower.

The scalding water was a pleasant relief to her aching body and the ability to get the dirt and sap off her body was an added bonus, but she knew getting everything out of her hair would be the most challenging. She knew that she wouldn't be able to get all of the dirt and sap from her hair, not without her own hair products, since her hair was so long and finicky, but she made due with what was there. She scrubbed as much of the gunk from her hair and body as she could and then closed her eyes to relax under the spray of the hot water for a little bit.

Grudgingly she knew she couldn't stay in the shower long; it was about time that she got things back on track and find a way to get home. Miya reluctantly shut the water off and stepped from the shower. She grunted at her dirty clothes and the thought of putting them back on just after getting clean. *'I'll just have to take another shower later,'* she thought, and redressed in her old clothes. After gathering all her things once again, she made her way back down the stairs to the kitchen.

"Would you mind if I borrow something to wear? My clothes are kind of done for," she asked, just after stepping back into the kitchen.

~*~*~

Alora's conversation with her husband didn't go as she had hoped, but at least she was in the loop now. Unfortunately, they were not able to come to an agreement on what to do about Micah's connection with the human.

"Sweetie..." Alora placed a hand onto her husband's hand, "you can't stop him from following his instinct. So you might as well start getting used to the idea that Miya is now part of this family. Besides, your son followed your rules. It might not be exactly how you wanted it, but at least it was done. All we can do now is just make sure that Micah and Miya understand what is going to happen in their lives from this point forward." Alora told her husband and he sighed heavily. This was not the way he wanted things to work out, but if this was what it was going to be, then he would just have to be fine with that...for now.

Both Alpha and Alora perked up when they heard Miya's voice.

"I'll get her something to wear, why don't you go check on Micah and maybe bring him some water," Alpha told his wife and they kissed before parting. Alora headed downstairs with a few things for Micah while her husband headed back upstairs to show Miya where she could find some spare clothes.

"We've got some clean clothes in the spare room; there should be something in there that you could wear. Everyone in the village is family by one means or another, so we all come and go as we please in each other's home, so some things get left here on occasion," Alpha explained to Miya as he led the way toward a spare room and began to trifle through a few drawers and the clothes. He sighed with relief when he found an outfit that looked like it would fit her small frame. **"This should work. If you find they are too small or too big, then you can look through the drawers and see if your size is there. When you are finished, then you can go to the basement. The door is down the flight of stairs and then just past the kitchen there is a steel door behind a wooden one. Alora should be down there now."** After that, he left without another word to go get himself cleaned up, so that he could be ready for the village feast tonight.

Miya was thankful that there was something else that she could wear besides her dirty clothes from running in the forest. She nodded her head at Alpha's words and waited until the man left before changing into the borrowed clothes. Miya made a mental note that if she ever got home that she could wash the clothes and return them somehow. Once she was satisfied with the borrowed clothes and her hair, she headed off back downstairs, following the directions Alpha gave her. After entering the kitchen, she looked around for the door that was described to her, still thinking it highly odd that a steel door would be hidden behind a wooden one and let alone one that led to a basement. She took a few tentative breaths, getting a foreboding feeling which caused her to glance over her shoulder towards the door she had been brought through earlier.

'It doesn't seem like anyone is around...I could run...' she thought and contemplated the success of running and actually getting away this time. She knew that it might not seem like there was anyone around, but if these people...creatures, were anything like actual animal wolves, then they probably had extraordinary hearing and smell.

'Fuck it.' Miya finally gave up the internal struggle and descended the stairs past the steel door. "Hello? Alpha said I could come down here to see about some wounds." She called as she took each step slowly.

~*~*~

Micah was thankful when his mother had brought down some water; but he wasn't really in the mood to eat something. "Mom, it's a bit difficult to eat when I'm chained," he groaned once again as she pushed a sandwich towards him.

"You know this is the best way we can deal with you when you get like this. Do you remember your first change?" She questioned him and he growled. She would always bring that time up.

"So I was the youngest one to shift since my great-grandfather and I just so happened to do it on the first blue moon in years and went nuts. How was I supposed to know how to handle it, just like right now? You and father never told me how strong this pull would be," he argued with her, though his sarcasm was probably not needed.

"There was no way for us to describe it to you but you didn't have to go and kidnap the poor girl. How do you think that made her feel, hm? Humans don't teach their children about us anymore, at least not the way they used to. Now we are monsters of the night who prey on young children to eat" His mother's voice sounded a bit resentful but she smiled at Micah when he rolled his eyes.

"Yes mother, I know the stories and I know I screwed up but she's-" Micah cut his sentence off when he heard Miya's voice and he craned his neck as much as the metal collar around his neck and the cuffs on his wrist would allow him. He felt his muscles relax the moment he saw Miya coming down and he sat back against the stone wall sipping at his water bottle.

"You are more than welcome down here Miya. I trust your shower was to your liking? Is there anything I can get you while I head upstairs to get Micah more water?" Alora questioned as she got to her feet to greet Miya.

"The shower was lovely, thank you again and no mam, I have everything I need in the first aid kit," she said, smiling towards Alora. Miya glanced towards Micah briefly, trying not to let her nerves get the best of her. Alora nodded her head with a smile on her face and headed back upstairs to give them privacy.

Miya had wished that Alora would have stayed but there was nothing she could do about that now so she carefully moved to stand in front of Micah giving an awkward smile. "Is it okay if I tend the wound on your shoulder? I also have some pain killers for your ribs," she said softly as she carefully removed her backpack from her shoulder and crouched down in front of the man. Micah stared at Miya; the girl was probably enjoying seeing him like this and was trying not to let it bother him. Instead he just smirked at her and nodded his head, allowing Miya to touch him as she pleased. Miya watched the guy's face closely, making sure she was welcomed before moving on to fixing up his wound and when she saw the slightly relaxed expression on his face she leaned in closer. Miya studied his face, took in his scent and tried to picture them together to see if she could feel this 'pull' that had been talked about. She had felt something when this man said that she was his one and only and that there would be no other but her. It felt nice to hear someone exclaim that about her, but she wasn't sure if that was enough. Miya knew this man

51

scared her; he was powerful and easily intimidating.

"I know what you are thinking," Micah stated as quietly as he could, his voice still came out deep and primal. "This is a normal thing for all children in the pack who are still growing and going through high intense times throughout life. It's more of a safety precaution for the others in the village and the humans in your town", Micah finally explained and swigged the rest of his water, then tossed the bottle next to him. He took a deep breath, letting Miya's scent fill his nostrils before he exhaled. Her natural smell was intoxicating and having his mate so close to him made him want to grab her and not let go. Instead, he just dug his fingernails into his bent knee to give him a bit of dull pain, helping him to resist doing as his body wanted him to. "Werewolf 101, we burn at a hotter temperature than humans and thus will burn through medication faster so I hope that your bottle of painkillers is big enough." Micah warned. He wasn't being mean or looking down on the girl, but since his mate was human, Micah felt that it was best that Miya knew a few things about his kind quickly.

Doisprezece

"So it's a way to make sure pups don't go around kidnapping people," Miya teased with a smirk and started to pull out peroxide and cotton pads to clean Micah's shoulder wound. A low growl emitted from Micah at Miya's jab to him, but that was quickly gone when the stench of the peroxide hit his nose. "Just a small warning, this is going to sting." She said while moving a bit closer to him and placed a hand on the part of his shoulder that was closer to his neck. Miya made sure to have an ample amount of cotton in her right hand while her left poured the clear liquid onto the wound and recalled how she had inflicted it. Micah wasn't so much bothered by the sting of the medicine as he was by the smell of the peroxide. He hated things that had an overly chemical smell but wasn't about to tell Miya that. Micah was happy that the girl was still willing to touch him.

Once Miya was satisfied with the amount of the liquid bubbling in the wound, she placed the bottle next to her leg. Miya remembered that most of her equipment for sewing a wound shut was back in her locker, and the best that she could do right now was her emergency kit of butterfly laceration bandages. Her hands trembled slightly the longer she touched him, and she knew that she should probably be worried right now, but her heart to help people kept those emotions down somewhat. "I'm sorry I don't have stronger pain killers but I guess you can ask your mother to get something for you" She said as she slowly started to close the wound, her dark eyes glanced towards the man's face for a second before returning to her task. "If I may ask, why are you against getting a wife here and just come to visit me now and again? Your father never said he would stop you from coming over, and maybe we could get to know each other." She asked out of curiosity once again and finished off fixing up his wound with some gaze and a wrap.

Micah's right eye twitched when his mate brought up the fact about him not wanting a wife from the village. Part of him was mad about the inquiry but mostly he was angered that she still couldn't understand...or more like, feel the same way about him as he did. When Micah got the chance, he grabbed Miya's wrist and yanked her closer to him, to the point their breath mixed. "You are my wife! I don't need anyone else and it hurts that you would even think about going along with what my father said!" Micah growled but this time it was a low, almost pained growl that turned into a whine before he released his grip on Miya and once again sat back against the wall.

Miya's eyes widened when she was grabbed, and she tried to rip her arm out of the man's grip, but it was useless, reminding her of the fear she held about this man. A mythological werewolf man who could snap her like a twig and force her into anything he wanted, most likely. Miya hardly heard the man's words about her being his wife and that he was hurt that she was even asking about him taking another woman. However, his actions continued to confuse her and when he emitted the pained growls and whines, it tore at her heart. She felt like she had just kicked a puppy. Though as quickly as she was grabbed, she was let go, stunned once again and staring at the man resting against the wall. She moved backwards a bit more, "there are two things wrong with your statement. One, I can't be your wife because if my family ever found out I was with a guy- a werewolf no less, they would hunt me down and kill me. Two, you scare the hell out of me, not because you are a werewolf, I can see you are not like the books or movies but because of what you can do. You can pick me up with ease. You have strength that I will never be able to fight against and probably many more abilities that I would never be able to compete with." She said as her fear showed on her face as she voiced her reasons.

'*That's it!*' Micah screamed in his head. He had tried to reason with the girl, being told that he scared her was the last straw. If he had known that this girl was going to be this difficult, then he would have just left her alone. Micah inwardly smirked to himself. If only he had been able to ignore the pull that he felt around this girl. Every time Micah acted on instinct, he scared her, but it was the words that pierced through him worse than any arrow or bullet. He could feel his heart being chipped away as he sat there chained to a wall, and it was starting to piss him off. "If I could just switch my feelings to someone else I would, but it doesn't work like that! If you are so worried about your family that you speak of and not your fated mate and since I scare you so much, then get out of here while you can!" Micah growled out this time, baring his teeth in threat towards Miya. He didn't want to believe his own words but right now he would rather deal with this pain than constantly being told that he was a fuck up and that his mate was scared shitless of him.

Miya jerked at Micah's sudden change in demeanor and worse those burning eyes that he turned on her chilled her down to her core. Micah's hands shot out seizing his opportunity of Miya still being so close and jerked upwards, standing as much as the chain around his neck would allow him with her in his clutches. "If you value your human life so much then get the hell out of here and don't even think of breathing a word of this!" Micah snapped directly in her face and then shoved her towards the stairs with half of his strength, still trying to protect her from as much physical pain as he could.

It barely took a second before his mother and father were flying down the stairs. Alora went directly to Miya while Alpha bolted straight for Micah and shoved him back against the wall. "Get her out of here. I don't want to see or hear her anymore. Let her return to her stupid human life!" Micah barked towards his parents. Alora's hands reached out for Miya, making sure she was alright before gently tugging her out of the basement.

"I'll close the door once we're upstairs hun," she told Alpha and he sharply nodded his head and then whipped it around to his son.

"What the hell has gotten into you?!" His father screamed to get his voice above Micah's growling.

Micah could feel his body starting to change even though he was trying his best not to shift. The chains hooked on him would only hurt more in his wolf form, though it could force the metal to bend slightly from the sudden transformation. He unfortunately was still thinking about Miya's wellbeing and if he caused himself any more pain then Miya would get it as well.

"You just found your mate and you are going to throw her away like that!" His father screamed at him only to have Micah jump at him. The chains stopped his attack but both of them could clearly hear the bolts starting to be pulled from their secured position.

"She doesn't want to be here and she's scared of me...I have no other idea of how to act around her," Micah snapped back at his father.

Alpha seemed to understand what his son was talking about but shook his head in disappointment anyways. **"No one ever said it would be easy. Even if your mate was one of us, it still wouldn't be easy. The fact you need to wrap your brain around is that your mate is human and needs to be cut more slack than normal."** His father explained in one of his signature calm tones.

He didn't want to hear his father's words right now, he had already figured most of this out but even if it wasn't going to be easy with one of his kind he still would have rather dealt with them because that way if they disagreed they would either yell at each other or start throwing punching to relieve the tension. Even females in the pack held their own and sometimes better than most of the men in the village.

Treisprezece

When Alora came rushing up to her she was confused. Part of her remembered why she should be terrified right now, but another part of her was hurt, this man was throwing her away after all the kidnapping, weirdly sweet words and the proclamation that she was his wife. She felt like she could get a crush on the guy if he wasn't so rough, but as it was, she was hurt both by being shoved and at how the man reacted to her honesty. Miya gave a weak smile and let Alora guide her out of the basement. She was still reeling from the sudden change in her talk with Micah and decided that it was best to sit down for a few minutes, especially since she was feeling a soft pulse around her joints and neck. She assumed that Micah was hurt by the chains.

"Can I ask you to tell me more about what happens when a wolf meets their mate?" Miya asked, wanting badly to understand. "He acts like he loves me even if he just met me, is that normal?" She questioned, feeling very lost.

Alora's brows creased, her heart went out to Miya, knowing that they had already set a bad example for the girl and seemed to be getting worse with every second. Alora sighed lightly after she closed and secured the basement steel door before turning to look at Miya again. She was impressed, however, that she was still here. Earlier, her husband had told her that Miya seemed to be trying everything under the sun to get away from them but here she was still asking questions.

Alora smiled at Miya and moved towards the nearest kitchen

counter to continue her prep work. "How about I ask you a question that might help clear things up a little more for you...why do you stick around asking questions about someone you don't understand or want to be around instead of taking your chance to get away from him?" She questioned, her tone was light with that all knowing motherly tone, and the smile to match. In no way was she being harsh, but Alora wanted Miya to realize that she had more of a connection with this place than she thought.

Miya shook her head at the question like she was trying to reject the reverse psychology Alora was pulling on her. Why didn't she run away, now given the chance? She didn't feel much different than when she was first kidnapped, scared and clueless, not to mention weak, but right now all she could think of was that whimper Micha did, and how pained he looked after Miya had told him the truth about her fears. "I guess it's because I hate seeing people in pain. When I told him the truth about my fears it looked like I had just kicked a puppy," she said, finally turning her downcast eyes to stare at Alora. "I also feel bad that the mate your son was promised ended up being a weak human. It must not be easy on him and seeing, as there is no way to break this bond, I feel sorry." She admitted, but it didn't look like Alora was believing a word she said, like there was something deeper there that Miya just couldn't figure out or didn't want to figure out. "Can you tell me about this pull Micah talks about? What does it feel like for him? Is everything that happened normal?" Miya continued to question, and then her eyes glanced over the prep work that was going on. She might as well help since she was just sitting there, most likely interrupting their plans.

Alora seemed happy enough by the way Miya spoke even if she didn't fully understand the feelings, but Alora kept her mouth shut at this point. 'At least she's sticking around,' she thought, and moved to another part of the kitchen, then briefly to the fridge before turning back to the girl. Miya was asking all the right questions for a human, but Alora was afraid that Miya wouldn't truly understand anything if she didn't feel it herself. "What Micah is going through is normal, maybe not for an alpha to be, but normal none the less. Unfortunately, he's dealing with it in every wrong way possible and I blame myself for that one. Micah was born solo and, being the handful he was, I couldn't even imagine having more pups at that time. His father had just become Alpha and I had been rescued by my husband after being cut off from my own pack for nearly a month, so there was a lot going on," Alora began explaining. It had been years since she thought of those days, even with some of them being sad and rough, she still loved remembering them. "Thank you for the help," she said, as a side note when she noticed Miya helping with some of the prep work for the feast, a smile beaming from her lips and then Alora moved to the side so that Miya could have more space to help with peeling the mound of potatoes that were on the counter. "Now what Micah is probably referring to when he says pull is the sensation his body feels when he's near you. Kind of like that first breath of life filling your lungs, though some have described it as two halves of powerful magnets finally snapping together when they are close....hm...well your pre-med right...I guess you could look at it like you just saved someone at the very brink of death, where everyone else has given up and you were the one to safeguard that person's life," she told Miya as she sat down on a nearby stool so she could rest her feet. "Does that help any?" She questioned, curious if she had explained it well enough for her.

Miya tilted her head while Alora finished speaking and was highly confused when Alora said she blamed herself for only having one child. "What does being an only child have to do with anything? And how does one normally deal with meeting their 'soulmate'?" She asked, wanting to get a baseline on the normal behavior of werewolves. However, her only child question dropped instantly when Alora described the 'pull' feeling. Miya was stunned and wondered if what Alora was saying was true because it seemed like such a powerful feeling wasn't really possible. She was having a hard time wrapping her head around such a feeling that could happen when they were around each other, yet it wasn't such an odd concept anymore that she was standing here peeling potatoes with her kidnapper's mom. She didn't imagine the type of feeling that Alora described but nothing seemed to spark. Maybe Micah's pull was off and she got cross in some kind of crossfire. *'Now that seems even more farfetched.'* She thought but could at least understand that Micah feeling something powerfully could send anyone into a frenzy. "Holy crap, I didn't realize that it was that strong, it must be hell for him right now then. And he'll feel this for the rest of his life. Damn, I shouldn't have said anything..." she frowned while glaring at a potato like it was at fault for everything happening the way it did. Miya wondered if there was any way that she could rectify the situation. After all, she wasn't a heartless person, just one that didn't really have the luxury of a relationship of any kind.

Alora could tell that Miya was cute and very sweet and she wanted to be able to give Miya a good place to go since she was Micah's mate, but she wasn't sure if anything positive was going to come from all of this if Miya was having such a difficult time grasping the small things about Loup Garou kind. Alora wasn't so sure of this pairing the more she talked with Miya and if nothing was going to come out of it she didn't want to get too attached. Alora shrugged her shoulders, "I'll explain about the only child thing at a later time. I don't want to bore you with details and my husband would probably go ballistic at how much I am telling you now. However, with the pull, each person's different. Some woo their mate, others feel the connection at the same time and cling to each other, while some, like Miach, react in extreme measures," she explained, and raised from her seat to get started on another portion of the prep work. "Oh and please don't feel too bad, he'll work things out eventually but don't forget about yourself as well. I'm sure all of this is very strange for you, after all the information on our kind, isn't the best it could be," Alora said with a smile on her face, trying to stay positive about this whole thing. Not that she was happy that her son's mate was human, that made her feel like a failure as a Loup Garou parent.

Alora walked up to Miya and rested a hand on her shoulder briefly before picking up a potato to help. "I can't apologize enough about how my son and husband brought you here, but please think of this place as a second home. I'm sure if you all decide to bring your bond to light, if you choose to accept Micah, that is, the pack will come around. Just know that you are always welcome here." She told her and turned her head slowly, hearing the basement door even as silent as it was, open, and then saw her husband coming up the stairs.

Alora swirled around quickly, "how is he?" She questioned with a worried look on her face and Alpha dropped his head slightly and shook it.

"He's calmed down to the point he's not going to shift but his anger is rising slowly at the fact that Miya is still here," Alpha explained just as he noticed Miya helping in the kitchen. **"Miya, if you want to return to the human town it'll have to be soon. The pack will soon be gathering in the courtyard for the feast tonight."** Alpha walked through the kitchen and slid onto a bar stool that looked over a countertop into the kitchen. Alora pushed the corn towards him, giving him a stern look until he started shucking the corn himself.

Miya was ready to brush Alora's apology off as not necessary anymore until Alpha came up the stairs, but she was just as eager to know how the man was doing and if he had done any more damage to his already beaten body that she had just fixed. Miya winced slightly when Alpha said that Micah was upset that she hadn't left yet. "I'm not sure I want to leave, I am still trying to wrap my head around all this, and I was hoping that Micah would at least have some patience after all." She stated but by the look on Alpha's face she was positive that he knew that it was a joke asking such a feat at this time. Miya pulled in a deep breath, hanging her head slightly since she still felt very guilty about the whole situation but obliged Micah's request this time. "I apologize for messing up your day but I guess it's better if I leave now." She announced just as she saw Alora making Alpha help with the prep work and even let a small snicker escape her lips despite feeling like crap. The two made an adorable couple and if Miya hadn't known any better she would have figured that they were just your average human married couple. "In all honesty it was a pleasure, Alora, I enjoyed talking to you a lot." She said, smiling at the women and then her golden eyes turned to Alpha "I am ready to go."

Alpha finished shucking the corn, and wiped his hands off on a nearby towel before pulling out his phone. **"I'll get Vin to escort you home. I would do it myself but I need to be here for the festivities,"** he explained while shooting Vin a quick message.

Patrusprezece

Alora walked up to Miya before she headed out and gave her a gentle hug. "You might feel the pull later or maybe you won't. It's not an exact science, but remember what I told you," she whispered into her ear, and returned to her business in the kitchen.

Alpha greeted Vin at the back door and he reported about the happenings in the pack and that everything would be ready for tonight. They both walked up to Miya, and Vin gave a giant smile, amazed that she was still in one piece. "You really did a number on Matt's head with that book of yours. He's got a giant lump on his head, it's funny really," Vin said, chuckling a bit before Alpha smacked him on the shoulder. "Oh right, gotta get you home..." Vin said and then led the way out the back door onto the lawn, not wasting anymore time.

Miya turned to Alora and smiled when she was given such a warm hug. She could not remember getting such a hug from her own mother for such a long time. She nodded to the women after returning the hug. "Could I get you to tell Micah that I am sorry everything got messed up? I feel horrible that I can't tell him myself, but as Alpha said, he was getting angrier the longer I am here," she said, with a hint of sadness that they couldn't work through this disastrous meeting. Miya gave a small wave before turning to greet Vin and remembering him from the tree and smiled a little, "Well that's what he gets for mocking my aim" she said with a light laugh to her voice, "but could you tell him I am sorry about that and I am willing to up hold my promise should he want a drink at some time."

Vin nodded. "I hope you are alright with speed and well...you know, because the fastest way for me to get you back to your town and make it back in time for the feast is for you to ride on my back." Vin said giving a slightly evil smirk but let it slip away as he crouched to the ground and letting the shift over take him. A stone-colored wolf now stood before Miya and Vin lowered his head to show that he was not going to cause the girl harm.

She stood in awe once again as yet another person transformed into a wolf before her eyes. It was such a mystery as to how they did it and why they were able to. Questions that would have to be answered later – if ever. Miya was still nervous at the thought of riding on the back of a wolf but she realized that she didn't have much of a choice if she wanted to get home and sleep. "Alright, just don't bite me," she said to the stone colored wolf after he bowed his head and then she moved around to his side "I am guessing like a horse?" Miya questioned but it was mostly to herself and awkwardly gripped the fur at the nap of Vin's neck just before swinging her leg up and over to sit on the wolf's back. "This is a little...well I'm not sure how to describe it," she commented and Vin snorted his irritated response. Vin didn't want to waste any time and launched into a fast trot before moving into a full run just to make sure that Miya wouldn't fall off.

As Vin weaved in and out of the trees he had to resist the urge to shake his fur at the weight upon his back. Vin's ears were standing high up, listening for anyone that might try sneaking up on them until he heard the noises of the town. Vin made sure to slow down gradually before coming to a complete spot and was more than happy to slide Miya from his back before shifting on the spot again, unconcerned with his bareness. "A bit of advice for you. If you feel bad for Micah, then you have one of two choices. One, don't ever set foot in our territory again, cut him off completely or two, don't apologize, get stronger mentally and stand next to him with your head held high as his mate regardless of species." Vin told Miya before pointing her in

65

the direction of the town. "Good luck with things," with that Vin shifted back to wolf form and headed off before the girl could apologize to him once more or apologize for doing something that was her own decision.

Miya shook her head, unable to even give a retort since Vin decided to shift and take off. *'What an asshat! How does he even know what's going on with me and Micah?'* She thought, her anger rising once more. Miya didn't like that these wolves knew more than they should and about private matters no less. With a heavy sigh she had nothing that she could do about it right now, so she began her trek back to her residence like nothing had happened in the last hours and happy that Vin had dropped her off closer to her home then she had originally been. Miya was glad to see her roommate was out, most likely at a party, and moved straight to her bed, stripping down to her underwear and donning her oversized sleep shirt just before diving under the blankets. Her schoolwork would just have to wait until tomorrow; her thoughts swam around her head as her eyelids began to get heavy, but even as tired as she was, it was hard to let everything go so that she could sleep. Getting fed up, she snatched her stereo remote from her nightstand to turn on some music in an attempt to block out her thoughts.

~*~*~

By the time Vin got back to the village, Micah was already out of the basement and walking around. Several people crowded him, asking questions about his injuries and Micah clenched his jaw and lied through his teeth. Vin looked at Alpha confused, but he was too busy greeting everyone and having small talk of his own. Vin walked straight up to Micah and placed a hand on his shoulder. "Do you think it's the best idea for you to be...you know," Vin hinted and Micah swatted the guy's hand off his shoulder.

"I'm just fine; it was just a little bump. No worries." Micah told his long-time best friend, but even Vin could see that Micah was pushing himself.

"Alright, if you say so." Vin stated, then jogged off to meet up with the other hunters.

The party started slowly, everyone gathering here and there. Soon food was being passed around. The pups were jumping on each other trying to see who could stay on top of the mountain of others the longest, the wrestling matches between the men started with a few females joining in and Micah wandered about the outer ring of the courtyard. He could feel a couple of eyes tracking his movements and could only take being closely watched for a bit until it became suffocating. Micah ended his night early, telling everyone that he was sorry but he wasn't feeling good. His mother helped him inside, giving him the option to sleep in his own room or to sleep in the basement.

Micah stared at his mother, blinking a few times. "I think I've spent enough time in that room to last me a while," he told her, but his eyes did linger over to the basement door. It probably would have been a better idea for him to go down there but his bed was much softer and thus won out his mental debate. Micah made his way up to the third floor and sauntered inside his room, making sure that his door as well as windows were tightly shut, not that it would probably stop him from leaving but it would at least cause a ruckus if he tried. He didn't even strip out of his clothes before plopping face first onto his bed and yanking his spare blanket up over himself before willing sleep to overcome him.

Cinsprezece

The next morning, Miya woke to the feeling of pins and needles throughout her body. Even stretching caused a hiss to escape her lips, but she was happy to find that she was in her own room. Miya pulled in a slow breath before sitting up. Part of her wondered if yesterday was a dream. Everything had happened so fast, her mind recalled faint images from her kidnap to pain, something about potatoes and a very large silver-shining white wolf that both fascinated and scared the shit out of her.

"Werewolves are real," she told herself and placed her forehead in his hands, still trying to grasp that reality. Still wrestling with her new reality, a soft chime sounded from her laptop "Right. Gotta get that pesky class work done" she huffed and pulled herself from the warmth of her bed, a few groans eliciting from her as she stood on her sore legs.

Miya's fingers flawlessly glided over her keyboard, checking her email quickly before pulling up her class work and the laptop chimed again. She switched to the group chat and found a few messages from a classmate about notes, Miya happily replied asking for any additional notes that her 'friend' had and they obliged. "That'll help," she commented softly to herself. Miya turned her attention to her assignments and decided that she would start with history first, since it was normally her hardest subject. Her legs bounced up and down, still trying to get rid of the tingling sensations, it was becoming a task just concentrating on her schoolwork. She tapped a pencil on the desk while moving between tabs of information.

Miya struggled through most of her homework but was only able to accomplish about two hours' worth before she couldn't take it anymore, painkillers weren't even helping. She decided it was time to have a much needed scalding hot shower with her own products. Miya quickly made her way to her bathroom, and was almost giddy at the ability to use her own shower. She was falling back into her normal routine but something felt off. Normally, her skin burning showers would always help to relax and rejuvenate her. Miya had always enjoyed her time alone but she couldn't help the lonely feeling that was growing in her heart. It was small before, like a tugging sensation, but it grew, making it hard for her to breathe. *'What the hell is going on?'* She thought, angrily shutting the shower off and getting out with a pissed growl.

Nearing lunch time, Miya had finally gotten situated in a clean outfit, hair done and an energy drink on her way out of the apartment. She had noticed by the front door was an extra pair of shoes. *'Roomie must have gotten lucky.'* She chuckled to herself. Miya wanted to relax, so she decided that lunch at club Luck Star would cheer her up. It had been a while since she was there, but one of the bartenders was probably the closest thing she had to an actual friendship since starting college.

Lucky Star was probably the only clean club and bar in town that didn't let its patrons get too out of hand and it had actual food. It was a very good place, the drinks were good, and the music wasn't so loud you couldn't think. The best part, the club was within walking distance of her residence. She slipped into the no-smoking section and sat comfortably in her favorite booth that faced the open set up of the place so that she could keep an eye on her surroundings. It was just something she always did.

It took a few minutes but she was able to finally flag down Jason, her bartender friend. "Hey Jason, how have things been since the last time I've seen you?" She asked with a small smile.

"It's been good. Haven't seen you in...damn, what's it been?

Weeks?" He joked with her and she punched his arm playfully. "Alright killa', easy. I still have a full shift to do. So want me to mix-up something for you?" Jason asked, his larger frame standing tall from Miya's seated form.

Miya nodded "That would be lovely Jason, and I would also like a burger and fries," she said, her smile growing a bit more. "Join me on your break, I could use the company," she called after him as he headed back to the bar and Jason nodded his head in response.

~*~*~

When the bright rays of the morning sun hit Micah's eyes he rolled over, tossing the blanket over his head and buried further into the bed. He had no intention of getting out of bed, his entire body ached, but the worst pain was the sensation of a red-hot fire poker slowly piercing his chest. Unfortunately, his father could be a strict asshole and today he was no different. The pounding on his door came not five minutes after Micah tried to go back to sleep.

"Get up Micah, you can't hold yourself up in there forever. Besides, your little clan of misfits is here..." his father chuckled. The nickname for his group started when he was just a pup. He and his friends were probably the oddest group in history. There was at least one person of every personality type they had: the nerd, the athlete, the joker, the rough-houser, the wuss, the reasonable one, the troublemaker and, of course, the muscle.

Micah listened for his father's footsteps to walk away from his room, but the pounding continued, **"Oh and don't forget you got some training duty today with groups two and three of the pups"**. His father called and Micah flung his pillow at his bedroom door. **"Don't make me come in there,"** his father warned in his alpha tone, it didn't really do much to him, since he also had alpha blood coursing through his veins, but still, coming from his father, it was annoying so he finally sat up in bed.

"Alright already. I'm getting up but I'm not doing any training today," he called back and listened as his father sighed heavily and then heard his mother lecturing his father about leaving him be, to deal with things on his own.

Micah took his time getting ready, though not to the point that he put on nice clothes; it was never a good idea to wear nice clothes unless his father ordered it for everyone, because you never knew when someone wanted to start a wrestling match. He fixed his hair up in his small dresser mirror before grabbing a light- well light for leather jacket- and slung it over his shoulder. He then quickly made his way downstairs hoping to avoid his father and almost got all the way to the front door before he was caught by someone.

"Keep your head about you out there Micah," his mother's voice traveled to his ears and he smiled. Micah turned to face his mother and embraced her in a tight hug.

"I will mother and thank you," he said before releasing her, and she smiled up at him while patting him on the shoulder. He cocked his head to the side when he saw a glint in her eye and was a little confused about it, but shrugged it off because he was already running late to catch up with the misfits.

Micah waved to his mother, opening the door just a crack, and at that moment he felt a hand grip the collar of his shirt as the door flung open and then his body lunged forward with force from a source behind him. His 'attacker' and he went tumbling out into the courtyard with a chorus of laughter following. Micah even started laughing as he was helped off the ground by Vin.

"Figured you could use a day filled with nonsense," Vin said, shrugging his shoulders, and Micah thanked his pack mates.

"So, what's the plan?" Micah questioned as the group pretty much led him into the forest, all with huge grins on their faces and to the average person that would look frightening, but for Micah that only meant one thing- they were going to be having some good ol' reckless fun.

"Well just as long as you don't think too much today, it's going to be a great day. First we are going to do some hunting up north in bear country so we are full and then after that it's time for some old school bar hopping," Matt explained, while a few of the others ran ahead, shoving each other playfully before shifting into their fur. Micah looked at Matt and Vin, the only two out of his group that knew what was really going on.

"Not sure if it's the best idea that I-" Micah started to say, but Vin pounded him on the back, cutting him off.

"Your father already gave us the go ahead. Like Matt said, don't think too much. Now come on before all the good game is taken by the others," Vin told him, and took off running. Matt shrugged to Micah, who still looked apprehensive about the plan for tonight. Him, drinking with thoughts of Miya still running through his head could prove disastrous.

"Come on Mic, just lighten up. She'll come around...eventually...maybe..." Matt said with a shrug of his shoulders, trying to help with his goofy little smile.

"Alright, let's go" Micah finally said, trying to sound upbeat, and soon took off after the others in a full out run. Matt wasn't too far behind him but he had to shift first just to keep up with Micah. Micah used a fallen log to launch himself through the air, enjoying the feel of wind on his face before shifting to feel the wind through his fur and hitting the ground with a thunderous thud that didn't even slow him down; not even feeling the impact of the ground on his paw because he was slowly feeling like himself again.

The boys ran nonstop from their territory in Bucharest to the border of Moldova before they stopped for a short rest and water before beginning their hunt. Four of the group members had already started hunting raccoon dogs, two decided to take on a group of wild cats but Vin and Micah took off to find something worth their time – brown bears. It took a bit to actually find a target for both of them but once they did, both wolves looked at each other and Micah winked at Vin before launching himself at the male while leaving the female for Vin. Vin was right behind him, growling in anger that Micah had beaten him to the male.

Once they were all finished eating, Micah led the group over to a stream so they could wash their fur off before lazing about the bank of the water. Everyone bounced around in small conversations here and there, but nothing really came of it. Micah had tried to trick one of the guys into telling him which bars they would be going to but they all just laughed before Vin shoved his shoulder with a paw and told him it was time to go.

Sasesprezece

Miya was finally relaxing and people-watching, while waiting for her food. It felt good to be around people even if she wasn't interacting with any of them and the loneliness she was feeling earlier began to subside until an odd sensation traveled up her legs that was followed by goosebumps. Miya rubbed her legs and the goosebumps seemed to go away. *'That was strange...there's no danger here...Micah?'* Miya wondered. *'This is going to get old real fast if I'm always going to have these weird sensations or pains,'* she thought with a bit of a sneer in her head. Miya was thankful when her food arrived because it gave her something else to focus on, which was the whole point of coming out. She didn't want to think about what had happened recently nor the fact that she was forever going to be bound to a werewolf.

"Mai Tai for you and a coke for me," Jason announced, before sliding into the booth closer to Miya than she would have liked but didn't point it out.

Jason laid his head on her shoulder with a heavy sigh, "I'm so tired of these afternoon shifts. It's always so boring," he mumbled with a yawn, and Miya rolled her eyes.

Jason always complained, no matter if it was an afternoon shift or a swing shift. She glanced sideways briefly watching Jason's brown hair fall over his eyes like he was trying to hide something, but she could clearly see him eyeing her lips as she sipped at her drink. Jason smiled when he noticed that Miya had caught him staring and he quickly sat up straight, clearing his throat.

'It's gotta be today before she doesn't come again,' he thought to himself while sipping his drink.

"So Miya, how's med school going?" Jason questioned and leisurely slung his arm around Miya's shoulders in an act of 'good buddy' just having fun with an old friend.

"It's been good. I finally got to treat an actual wound yesterday, so that was fun," she stated after rolling her shoulders until Jason moved his arm onto the back of the booth.

"So, how's your boyfriend? Haven't seen him around like usual," she commented and made a point to look around again, in hopes of catching the bleach blonde boy. Jason's boyfriend was at least a funny guy and could liven up the mood easily, but Miya couldn't find him anywhere.

Jason cringed, "A...we broke up about a month ago, but you know it was his loss anyway. Lucky for me, I have a very wide dating pool since gender isn't really a criteria for me. Besides, I have my eyes on someone" he said, smirking a little, and Miya scooted just a tad bit away from him. She hoped that he remembered that she was not up for dating and the fact that Jason was a better friend for her than a boyfriend.

~*~*~

Micah had lost count of how many bars they had gone into after counting six. At each one they had about two drinks before moving on. It wasn't the alcohol that made it hard for him to keep track, it was the fact that he was tired of trying to keep track.

"Alright Mic, this is the last one. We need to be able to walk tomorrow so don't go overboard," Matt told Micah as Vin pulled him into the bar.

Micah was able to look up at the bar sign just before he was pulled inside. "Lucky Star, really guys" he grumbled, making the others burst out laughing. Micah wasn't sure how much fun they would be having here, since Lucky Star was mostly known for a different type of crowd.

"Hey, if we get hungry there's food too," one of the others commented and Micah just shoved the guy.

"You're always eating dude," he said laughing as they all walked up to the bar and sat down.

"Bartender! A round of the strongest shit you've got!" Vin called out, pointing to the group.

~*~*~

Jason was about to make his move on Miya when a rowdy bunch of guys came filing in and he was needed at the bar. He groaned but gave Miya a small apologetic look before sliding from the booth to return to the bar, Miya's scent heavily clung to his side from sitting so close to her.

"Hello boys, just a sec and I will have those made for you," he said, counting each head and starting to mix up the drinks for each of them. His brown hair and gray blue eyes looked at each of them with a smile while he concocted the strongest drink they had and poured an equal amount of the contents into each glass.

The boys were glad that it didn't take long for their drinks and several of them had started flirting with the bartender the moment they saw him. Micah, on the other hand, was having a hard time swallowing and the fire in his chest earlier that morning came back with a vengeance; the tightest it had ever been. Once Micah got his drink, he downed it fast. Fortunately, Vin was the only one that noticed and was concerned.

"You might want to chill out man, you know that's not the best way to get drunk," Vin said a little too loudly and Micah turned his pain-torn eyes to him.

"I can't help it. Something feels off," he said and snatched up Vin's drink as well. "I gotta get rid of this tightness," he finally admitted when he got closer to Vin, so he would be the only one to hear.

Vin glanced around the place, his eyes threatening to go wide as saucers when they landed on Miya who was slumped down in a booth and hadn't spotted them yet. The boys were trying to get Micah's mind off the girl, not throw it in his face.

"Hey Matt, why don't we have a round of pool?" Vin called out to the guy from across the bar and received a funny look. Vin nudged his head to the side towards the table Miya was at and the realization came to his buddy's face.

"Yeah that sounds like fun. What do you say, Micah?" Matt quickly asked, only to see Micah shake his head no. "Oh come on. Bet you I can sink the eight ball faster than you..." he tried, but it didn't seem like he was going to take the bait.

Micah then turned to Matt when he could clear his mind off his chest. "$100 and you take my training groups for a week." Micah made a deal and Matt groaned loudly until Vin stepped up.

"Deal. But if you lose you owe us each $200." Vin said and they shook on it.

"Alright. This is going to be some easy money," Micah said, and he was led in the opposite direction of where Miya was sitting while leaving the others to continue their flirting with the bartender.

Jason flirted back as all bartenders should to get more tips. He was enjoying the attention from the group but his mind kept wandering back to Miya waiting for him in the booth; his eyes turned to look to see if Miya had run off yet and was happy to see she was just enjoying the music along with her food. His attention shot back to the group at the bar when he barely caught sight of a man downing his entire drink like it was a shot. Jason quietly alerted the other bartenders to keep an eye on the man that had taken his drink like a shot and to cut him off if he got too drunk.

When his tasks at the bar were completed once again, Jason started to make his way back towards Miya but only got halfway there when he saw Miya slip from the booth and head off towards the only set of restrooms by the pool tables. He sighed heavily and reluctantly headed back to the bar for now.

"Alright boys, should I make you cry now?" Micah said, finally feeling like himself again as he watched Matt rack the balls. He was just glad that his buddies still hadn't learned a thing about playing pool with him.

"Oh, I think it's Matt who's gonna make you cry," Vin said, laughing, and both boys looked at the other guy. Matt just seemed to smile nervously, he wasn't a bad pool player but he knew that Micah was so much better than him.

"Oh you think so. Well then how about we raise the bet?" Micah questioned with an evil grin on his face and Matt's face went completely white.

"Hell no!" Matt blurted out and Vin slapped him on the back.

"Come on Matt, Micah's not that good. How about we make it $300 a piece?" Vin questioned.

"No way. You play Micah if you think you are so good!" Matt blurted out and shoved the pool stick at Vin. "I am not going to drain my savings because of you two knuckleheads" Matt yelped and Micah busted out laughing.

"Well, if that's the case then sit and watch me kick his ass," Vin said with a smirk and waved to Micah to crack the balls.

"You are going to regret those words..." Micah lined up his shot, "and I'll take that bet" he said, his grin spreading across his face more. He pulled the pool stick back, aiming his shot and just when he was about to actually take his shot he froze. *'Can't be...'* he thought to himself, trying not to let his jaw slack when he caught sight of a familiar scent wafting from some beautiful black hair. *'There's no way Miya is here,'* he thought, his hand still frozen right as he was taking his shot until Vin stepped into his field of vision.

"Well, are you going to take your shot or what Mic? Don't tell me you are scared and going to back out now" Vin harassed him and Micah shook his head from side to side to clear his thoughts. Micah assumed that since he wanted to see her so badly, that he was just imagining that Miya was there.

"Hell no I'm not gonna back out. I was just thinking, how about we double the bed?" He challenged and Vin waved him on, accepting the bet.

Saptesprezece

Miya was glad when she made it to the restrooms without a problem like a drunk running into her or being cornered by a drunk and hit on. Even though it was the afternoon, there were still several people out who apparently didn't have a work life. Her golden eyes looked at herself in the mirror and tried to see what someone like Micah would see in her. She couldn't get her mind off of the guy. He looked like he could have his pick of a girlfriend – hell probably every female in a ten mile radius was jumping to be his wife but her...what was so good about her that she would get paired with a mythological creature. Miya was average at best. She was smart but her sarcasm usually got in the way and prevented her from having any sort of meaningful connection with anyone. Miya ran a hand through her hair, sighing heavily in frustration, before turning towards one of the stalls.

Her lonely feeling was starting to come back, even splashing water on her face didn't refresh her and this time she refused to look at herself in the mirror before exiting the restroom.

Back in the crowd of bar goers, she still felt like something was off. *'Looks like it's time for another drink,'* she thought to herself and slowly weaved through the crowd back to her booth. Miya sat heavily once she was back at her table and waved Jason down, tapping her glass in a way of asking for another. She smiled in thanks when Jason quickly came over with a new drink for her and sat back down. "Saw some guys flirting with you. Any of them catch your fancy?" She inquired with a smirk.

Jason laughed and shook his head. "They were nice, and I do flirt a lot, but that's just for tips," he said, grinning as he moved to lean against Miya lightly. "But the person I am looking to have is much sweeter, a bit too smart for their own good and sometimes a little too reserved." Jason said, turning his head just right to brush his lips against Miya's cheek before his hand moved out to grip Miya's jaw and turned her face just enough to pull Miya into a deep kiss, going so far as to bite at her lower lip to mix a little pain with the pleasure.

Miya froze when Jason kissed her, her mind buzzing with so many things at the act and when her lip was bit she gasped, giving Jason enough time to thrust his tongue into her mouth. Miya quickly shoved Jason away from her and glared.

"Holy fuck Jason! I've told you before, I am not looking to date and if I was it wouldn't be you," she hissed while touching her now throbbing lip.

Jason pouted when he was pushed. "Right, Sorry Miya... but just think about it? Please?" He asked softly and stood up to return to work.

Miya huffed out once Jason was gone, she felt like shit. Her lip stung and now there was an immense pain in her chest, like she was being clawed from the inside out.

~*~*~

The pool game started out well, at least Vin was a better challenge than Matt was, but it was still easy money for him and soon that money would be going to good use. Micah had his eye on this particular motorcycle for quite some time, though there were also a few other things that he needed money for. His parents thought he was crazy to want a motorcycle, asking questions about why he would want one when he was faster in wolf form than almost anything. However, he always shook off their questions, telling them that they would never understand.

Micah looked at his second to last shot and sank the ball with no problem, standing briefly before realizing that he only had the 8 ball left. "Looks like that $600 is going to be mine," he jabbed at Vin, who didn't seem too worried, but that was Vin, he usually always stayed cool under pressure. Micah lined up his shot, his eyes darting to Vin's face right in his way and he smirked. He pulled back the pool stick and launched it at the cue ball, but just before he made contact with the back, a searing pain ripped through his bottom lip, forcing him to jerk backwards, clipping the cue ball and launching it towards Vin's head.

"SHIT!" Micah screamed as his hand flew to his lip to brace the pain. Vin quickly stepped to the side while his eyes followed the ball and watched as it was buried into the wall.

Both Vin and Matt looked over to him. "What the hell was that for?" Vin snapped, feeling like Micah had done it on purpose.

"Hey don't look at me. I was about to kick your ass and get that money and then it felt like someone clocked me in the mouth," he explained to them, and then his own words hit him. Micah immediately started looking around the bar. "I wasn't seeing things, was I?" He growled, turning his eyes to his friends when he couldn't find his intended target. Matt immediately started backing up, which left one person for Micah to grab, Vin.

"She's here, isn't she!?" He barked at his friend, baring his teeth and his eyes burned with anger at that moment.

"Look, I didn't know she was going to be here," Vin said, putting his hands up.

"But you did realize it. How long did you know she was here?" Micah snapped at him and watched as Vin shrugged his shoulders.

"We're leaving, bet's off," he said, shoving Vin's back into the wall and stalking back towards the bar. As Micah walked by his pack mates, not caring about the scene he was making, he slapped each one of them on the back quickly "We're out, now!" He barked out, making everyone jump off their stools and quickly following behind him and out of the bar.

"Dude, what the hell was that all about?" One called as they all caught up to him.

"Yea I was about to get it with that bartender," another spoke but Vin and Matt motioned for them to chill out.

~*~*~

Miya jumped when she heard a loud scream and something thudding hard. Much like everyone in the bar, she stood to see what was going on but, unlike everyone else, Miya was looking to see if someone was hurt or not. After all, she had the training to help if needed. She was shocked to see an 8-ball ball embedded into the wall and then some familiar faces appeared in the crowd. *'What are they doing here? Should I leave?'* She thought, but even her thoughts froze when she saw a very pissed off Micah. She was struck with the sensation to be near him, to soothe him, but she couldn't bring herself to move at that moment. When she heard Micah shouting that they were leaving, Miya's body acted on instinct and before she knew it she was blocking the exit to the bar.

When Miya saw Micah heading her way she swallowed and steadied herself. "Micah...um...if it's not too much trouble...could we talk? Alone?" She asked in her most diplomatic tone she could muster, otherwise she was going to sink away from the heat of anger that was rolling off of him. Miya stood there, staring up at Micah and realized the closer he got the lonely feeling left. *'Is this the pull Micah and his family talked about?'*

Vin and Matt exchanged looks when Miya stopped Micah. They were waiting for the yelling to start or maybe Micah would just sidestep her and walk away. The others in the group were dumbfounded and they would remain that way, however. Matt shoved a couple of them out the door and passed Micah and Miya when they asked Micah how he knew the girl.

Micah's eyes were trained on Miya the entire time, he wasn't exactly mad...OK, he was slightly mad, but the urge to reach out and grab Miya to embrace her in a hug was stronger. He wanted to apologize for his behavior yesterday and tell her that if he could do it over he would, but that would make him look weak. Micah took a deep breath, his eyes stayed trained on her face but the last words spoken to him by Miya rang loud and clear in his head, 'you scare the crap out of me', they repeated over and over every time he took a shallow breath standing there staring at her.

"Mic, dude, come on," Vin said, placing a hand on his shoulder and pushing him a bit. Micah punched his friend's hand away.

"Don't touch me," he growled at the guy, turning his eyes onto him for a second before looking back at Miya. "Get out of here Vin, I don't want the misfits getting any stupid ideas. I'll meet up with you at the forest edge," Micah told his buddy without even looking at him, but he could sense Vin's hesitation before moving past him and taking off after the others.

Micah rolled his shoulders to relax himself before he cracked his neck from being so tense, and set his eyes onto Miya's face. She was far more beautiful than he had first thought and his eyes memorized every inch of her face until he saw the red mark marring her beautiful lips. "We can't talk here," Micah mentioned softly. He already felt the eyes on him the moment he had headed for the door and apparently no one had anything better to do than stare at them.

"I know where we can talk," she said and grabbed Micah's hand. Micah jerked slightly but before he could pull his hand away, Miya was already dragging him through the crowd towards the back of the bar. They emerged from the back door into the alleyway, it didn't smell the greatest but they could get some privacy there. At most, there would be a drunken couple making out. Miya turned to look up at Micah when the back door closed. Micah was thankful when they made it to their intended destination quickly and he quickly took his hand back.

"Let me start by saying I'm sorry about what I said. It's been bothering me and as your parents told me, this whole mate and pull thing is a hard thing to navigate...would you be willing to get to know each other at least? I know I pissed you off the last time we talked and I'd hate to do that again." She said softly, feeling a bit of pain in her lip the more she talked, but just being near Micah her lip didn't hurt as much and her chest didn't have that gripping loneliness anymore.

Micah stared blankly at Miya, hearing everything she said, but had a sarcastic remark sounding off in his head to everything she was saying. *Why should I care what this girl thinks? Not to mention why does she even want to apologize to me for what she said? Thought I scared her.* Micah knew that it was proper for a human to be scared of his kind, and that Miya shouldn't want to talk to him or be near him, yet here she was standing a back alley where he could probably get away with doing whatever he wanted and she was just talking to him.

His eyes drifted to Miya's lips once more, feeling his own throb from the abuse, and then his brain clicked into action leaving Miya's words unanswered. "Who bit your lip?" He questioned with a bit of a rough tone to his voice, feeling his possessiveness rising up and at the moment he didn't want to ignore it. Someone had clearly left that mark on his mate and caused her pain. Micah was going to find out who did it and make sure they got it through their head that they would not be doing it again. Micah quickly thought over his actions and words before shaking himself. "What I'm saying- screw it, you know why I'm saying it. Tell me who bit your lip and I'll agree to this whole 'getting to know each other' thing," he finally spit out, figuring that since he already scared the crap out of his mate, that he might as well actually do his best to make sure he was the only one to scare the girl or leave marks like that on her. Besides, Miya already knew how he could get, so this should be nothing new to her.

Optsprezece

Miya blinked when the conversation changed suddenly to her lip, and she brought her hand up to touch the redden lip before wincing. "Ah, that. Well, a friend of mine thought it would be a good idea to confess his feelings for me with a rough kiss." She said, not dropping any names at the moment because she could tell with the roughness of Micah's voice that he wanted to do something bad to Jason. "It's nothing really, I told him no and he went back to work, though its most likely going to be awkward hanging out with him now," she said shaking his head a little and then nodded her head when Micah said she knew why he was asking the way he was, after all Miya was a pretty smart person. "That compromise is not exactly even and I will only tell you the name if you promise that you won't hurt him. Alright?" She compromised, being the stubborn person she was.

To lighten the growing tension Miya lightly touched Micah's arm. "I don't need someone defining my honor, I can do that myself," she said giving what she hoped was a cute smile because she wasn't very well versed in that aspect of being a girl.

Micah went from being on edge to actually furious. Miya was not going to tell him the guy's name because she thought she could defend herself. He also didn't like the idea that Miya wouldn't let him do something about it even though it was his right. Micah calmed down a little bit when she touched his arm. That small act actually made him feel better. However, he was not going to let this slide. Not only did this person bite his mate, but it affected him, and this guy had the gull as Miya's friend to do that to her. Micah's eyes tracked his mate's face, replaying all of her words and gawked. His mate was still going to hang out with the bastard even though he bit her.

Micah pulled in a steady breath of air through his nose. "You've already given me enough information. I don't like the fact that you won't let me protect you, however, I have no right to fault you on that-for now, and I will agree to getting to know you but I will not agree to going easy on the bastard." Micah growled out in the calmest manner he could muster and then turned hot on his heels back into the bar.

Miya raised a brow when Micah looked her over and then gawked, she should have known better to not give so much information; really it was stupid of her to think Micah wouldn't pick up on things. "Oh no you don't! Leave him alone, I already told him no. I don't need a mate to go up to him and fly off the handle." She said gripping Micah's leather jacket, attempting to either stop him or slow him down but her grip faltered when he took a sharp turn, charging back into the main area of the bar.

Micah didn't want to waste any more time, and once back in the bar, he quickly scanned the place. '*Someone who is Miya's friend, so that means Miya's scent will be on the guy, and this guy has to be working here if he immediately went back to work.*' Micah thought and closed his eyes while taking a deep breath. He ignored where Miya's scent was the strongest. It took a bit for Micah to zero in on the guy because of all the scents that hung in the air of the bar but when he was able to pinpoint the exact person, Micah stalked up to the bar and barely leaned over the bartop to grab the collar of the guys shirt while yanking him halfway over to him so he was right in the bastards face.

Jason had been walking back and forth behind the bar, filling drinks as they came up and making small talk, which died immediately when he saw a guy stomping towards the bar. Jason's brows knitted together. He hoped that nothing major had happened and put on a smile nonetheless. However, Jason's smile dropped from his face like a lead weight when the guy yanked him over the bar to the point they were nose to nose. Jason clawed at the hand gripping his collar to try and pry the man's fingers off of his shirt; several people in the bar began to chant 'fight, fight'.

"Oi! If you have a problem, take it outside, not in the bar asshole." He glared at the man, standing his ground as best he could even with his feet barely touching the actual ground.

Miya was just moments behind the action and came to the sight of Micah and Jason with shock painted on her face. *'Knew something like this was going to happen,'* she thought and pushed through the crowd to get to the two. "Micah, let Jason go. He didn't do any harm, " she actually pleaded this time.

Micah smirked not even hearing Miya's words because of everyone else in the bar calling out for him to start a fight and if his buddies had been here then they would have been right behind him waiting for the word to help. "Alright then let's step outside," he growled to the guy that had balls enough to speak to him like that, still ignoring Miya. Micah was ready to pick the guy up and chuck him through the closest door or window to get him outside so that he could kick his ass.

Micah finally turned his sights onto Miya when she stated that the guy didn't do harm to her. "No harm?! Look at your lip and tell me that he didn't do any harm!" Micah snapped at Miya and returned to his business with this Jason guy. "I will not give you another opportunity to hurt Miya. Your luck ran out the moment I stepped in this bar. So the next time you think with your dick, remember me and how badly I kicked your ass." Micah growled at the guy and it came off a little more predatory this time then he had meant it to be. With that, Micah dragged the guy over the bar, not even allowing him to stand on his own feet and did what the guy told him-Micah headed outside to beat the crap out of him.

"Micah, stop this right now. You are making a scene. Don't do this, show me you can be better than this," she stated and followed closely behind, pounded on Micah's back, not that it did much. Miya could see the surprise on Jason's face when Micah pulled him over the bar like he weighed nothing. Jason was also trying to get a swing on Micah as he was dragged towards the bar entrance. Jason hoped that someone was calling the cops right now.

"I didn't hurt Miya! I was just telling her how I felt, dammit! She doesn't even have a boyfriend so why are you acting like a fucking caveman!" Jason screamed and was finally able to get Micha's hands off him so he could stand on his own feet.

"Caveman! Why is it always caveman?!" Micah growled, so not only did Miya sock him in the gut with her comment about being better but this guy Jason had the balls to do it to. Micah sighed heavily, his brain agreeing with Miya's point, though his heart still spurred him to kill this fucker. Micah knew that he was better than this and apparently as the guy put it, Miya didn't even have a boyfriend. But he was not going to let all the comments slide, he had his pride to defend at least and with a quick jerk of his hand Micah gave a half powered punch square in Jason's face, and leaving the bastard to deal with the pain and broken nose. "You win Miya, if he's that good of a friend. I've got to get back before the others wonder too much." He told Miya even though he still radiated anger and even had to stop himself after he took a few more steps towards Jason to continue. He was still peeved that this stupid horny bartender got to kiss his mate and he could barely touch the girl without the fear of scaring her.

Micah took a deep breath and ran a hand through his hair before giving up the fight with himself and finally leaned closer to Miya, giving her a small kiss on the cheek. "Until next time," he said softly only for Miya to hear before bolting out the back door.

Nouăsprezece

Micah made sure not to run into anyone as he slid into the alleyway, but when he cleared the opening of the alley he had to jump sideways to avoid a car and had to quickly roll back onto the sidewalk to avoid getting hit. He normally would have already shifted but he was too far in town still to do that and he could hear sirens from police cars getting closer, no doubt because of the commotion he caused in the bar. That was the last thing he needed to deal with, but at least tonight he could chalk up a victory with Miya. She had even managed to slip something into his hand before he had taken off. He thought he was fast, but somehow she was much sneakier than he had first thought she could be.

He skidded to a halt just barely inside the brush of the forest, a few of his pack mates were already shifted and roughhousing with each other while Vin stood off to the side with his arms crossed over his chest.

"That took far too long," were Vin's first words when Micah came to a stop.

"Well a few things happened that were out of my control," he said, shrugging his shoulders and watching as Vin's eyes widened.

"Please for the love of the moon you didn't slaughter the girl?" Vin exclaimed and Micah just chuckled.

"Nope. Better," but that was all he was going to say. "Come on, let's get back home, I'm beat." Micah said as he stretched and let a yawn pass his lips. The group eyed him for a moment before they all nodded their heads and took off running for the village.

As they neared the village, the group shifted back except for Miach, he was still feeling too excited to leave his fur. Micah barked to the others as he headed off to his house, nudging the door open with his nose before slipping into the building.

"I don't think so young man, your paws are going to track dirt everywhere," his mother's stern tone hit his ears and he laid them flat on his head. "You shift right now and go take a shower then you better get some sleep because you have training tomorrow," she told him and he quickly shifted, gave her a peck on the cheek and bolted upstairs.

~*~*~

Micah's morning started much more pleasantly than previously because this time his father wasn't pounding at his door and he was able to slowly wake with the rays of the sun just barely peeking over the horizon. He followed his normal routine for the morning, feeling almost like himself again since finding his mate, but it was still there in the back of his mind. Micah joined his parents in the nook for their morning meal and then took off shortly before his parents' finished. He had about three hours to do his own morning workout before getting to the pups. He was still unsure of what he wanted them to do today because all Micah could think about was the tiny crumpled piece of paper that Miya had shoved into his hand yesterday.

Even during his morning workout in the forest, his mind drifted towards that paper with Miya's number on it, something he didn't even think that he would be privy to for a long time, since he screwed up the initial meeting. Micah wrestled with his own thoughts as he bounded through the forest. He had made a point to cut the girl out of his life the moment she spoke of her fear of him, but now it seemed as though Miya wanted something to do with him for the moment. It was going to be a very tricky path between them and Micah worried he'd step on another landmine.

Micah cut his workout short because he was unable to fully concentrate, so instead he returned to the village where his two training groups were already waiting for them. All the eager pups stared at him, and were waiting to be told what to do. He shifted back to human form after a few minutes, staring at the pups and making sure everyone was in attendance, then he patted all of them on the head. "Alright pups. So far, you have all done your individual training, but now we are going to start your group training. These groups will become your lifeline from now on, as well as your hunting parties. You are required, whenever asked, to assist one another whenever they need help, so I suggest you learn to get along." Micah began explaining the basics and then continued on the tasks that each group would need to complete before sending them off.

While the groups were off completing their tasks, Micah bounced up to his room to grab his cell phone and sent Miya a quick message so the girl could at least have his number as well. Before waiting for a reply, Micah bolted back out of the house, shifting once he hit the courtyard and then went hunting for his training groups.

Micah was careful about how close he got to his training groups while stalking them. He circled one of the groups for a bit before pouncing on one of them from the rear. He turned the pup over on his back before going after another one. From there, the group scrambled out of formation with a few bolting off.

'Get back to your group!' He called out to them and quickly took off to find the other group.

Yet again he repeated the same attack of jumping on one of the pups. However, this group seemed to be a little better. Two of the pups circled around him while he had one on the ground and the others jumped on his back. Their small teeth gripped onto the scruff of his neck to hold him, one shook his head, forcing Micah to release the one he had captured.

Training kept up like this until he called all the pups together and they went back to the village. "Some of you did well today, while others still have things to work on. If you can help it, never split from your group. If you were to be caught on your own, it would be disastrous. Also, you NEVER leave your packmates behind to be slaughtered. The rest of you also need to be aware of the fact that even the most calculated plan by one person can be disrupted. You all know what you need to work on, so get some rest and then work on it," he dismissed them.

Micah yawned into the back of his hand as a gentle throb pulsated from the back of his neck. "Man, those pups can have some sharp teeth," he commented as he walked into the kitchen to grab a water bottle.

"I assume training went well today?" His mother asked as he sat down at the counter.

"You could say that. They still have a lot to work on but they learn fast," he commented, and watched his mother point to his phone.

"It went off a few times," she commented, and returned to her own task. Micah thanked her and snatched his phone off the counter, reading the messages before he headed up to his room.

Since he was free of pack duties now, he might as well get started on this 'getting to know each other' thing that Miya wanted to do. Plopping down on his bed, Micah dialed Miya and listened to it ring a few times before hearing the call go through. "What's up? Sorry for the lateness. I had a training group to work with today." Micah admitted in a clear cut tone like he was just talking to one of his buddies instead of like he was talking to his mate even though deep down he wanted to treat her differently. He should have the right to act like Miya was special to him, but knew that the human had her doubts already about him.

Douăzeci

Miya reluctantly sat up in bed when the bright sun barged through her window. She wasn't ready for another round of classes like she usually was. It was a bit hard to get motivated about school now that she had encountered something unheard of in normal society. "Urge," she groaned and forced herself from the warmth of her comforter and trudged around her room getting ready for her early morning classes. She was questioning herself the entire time why she even wanted to be in the early morning group? Miya glanced at her phone, '*6:30 am, too fucking early,*' she thought to herself and began to slip into lose fitting pair of jeans today and a tangtop. She bounced from side to side of her bedroom, making sure she had everything she would need for the day, and snatched her phone from her nightstand along with her favorite hoodie. With one last glance at her cozy inviting bed that she wished she could have stayed in until noon, but she couldn't, so she darted from her residence. While bounding down the steps she remembered that it was Friday and her steps gained a bit of bounce to them.

Miya was also excited about it being Friday because that meant that she was going to get to see her favorite teacher. Her favorite professor was a lively woman who loved her job and loved to teach and always made class time so entertaining. The woman really did know how to keep her students engaged in her lessons.

~*~*~

"Finally," Miya sighed with relief that classes were over and labs were done. Now she was quickly on her way back home to drop her things off before heading into town. She had been looking forward to some relaxing time of window shopping and a nice strong mocha. As she continued on her way home, she noticed a group of people ahead of her. She knew some of them from class, but she never did talk much with the other students unless needed. She briefly imagined what it would be like if she was friends with anyone and what hanging out would feel like with so many people. Fully into her daydream now, she closed the rest of the distance to her place and just getting inside the front door her phone buzzed. It confused her because usually the only time she got any kind of communication was with her family or her professors. She stared down at the message, stunned. Micah had actually texted her. The message wasn't anything glorious, just a simple ~hi, how are you? It's Micah.~ And that was it. *'Well, at least he texted,'* she thought, and sent just as much of a generic response as he had and saved his number in her phone.

Miya didn't stick around home that long, she was looking forward to her day out. *'I should try to be a little more...'* she couldn't think of the words but she just knew that she had to try like they both had agreed at the bar. She sighed heavily and pulled her phone from her back pocket ~Why don't you give me a call later and we can discuss a few things.~ She hesitated with a finger over the send, she felt a bit silly sending a message like that but any way that she phrased it in her head sounded even cheesier. "Oh fuck it," she said to herself and finally sent the message. Miya still felt really awkward about the whole werewolf mate thing. Hell she felt awkward just knowing that someone was this into her and she had no clue how to handle it.

Throughout the day after the text, Miya felt like little needles were pricking her skin. It was light, so it only slightly bothered her, but she wondered what the hell Micah was doing at the moment that would be causing these strange pinpricks. She rubbed the back of her neck where it tingled the most. Miya ended up cutting her outing in town short from the odd sensations and found herself back home once again. She tried everything to relax, even procrastinating on her homework and defaulting to her earbuds to listen to her favorite music while lounging on her bed. With another round of buzzing from her phone she audibly groaned, pretty ticked that her alone time was being interrupted yet again. "Hello? This better be important," she stated, without even looking at the caller ID, and when she heard Micah's voice her heart jumped into her throat.

"Oh fuck," she whispered away from the phone, glad that Micah seemed to brush past her rude greeting. "No worries. How was training?" She cleared her throat, trying to relax as Micah touched on his day. She rubbed the back of her neck a little more, the needle feeling still there. "Did you hurt the back of your neck or something today? You should probably put a cool cloth on it or something, because if I can feel it, then it must be bothering you, if I'm not mistaken," she said, and laid against her pillows. Miya heard Micah chuckling at the comment about the neck pain.

-I forgot about the fact that you would feel the pain. I'll try to be more careful.-

She heard him as it sounded like he was shifting around.

-Honestly, the pain isn't that bad for me. The pups just have sharper teeth when they are in wolf form and I was running an ambush drill with them today.- Micah explained softly. -Sorry about that.- He apologized just so it was out there, though he really didn't need to because it wasn't like he could give up on his duty to the pack. She listened to his explanation about the pups and their teeth and chuckled to herself this time.

"Ah, that explains it," she grinned. "Um...so should we...have a do over of that first meeting tomorrow...if you're free that is? I know this garden that we can walk around and talk," she said, thinking that Micah would like being around nature more than anything else.

-The garden sounds nice though, depending on what we are

going to talk about, if there are too many people around I would rather not discuss things about the pack- Micah told her as a soft yawn crept up on him.

"Right, how about we walk around the forest?" Miya suggested and she heard a confirming grunt from Micah. *'He must be tired.'*

"Alright so tomorrow late morning, there's a lake about half a mile north of campus into the forest. I'll meet you there," she stated, and heard another confirmation before they said their goodbyes for the remainder of the evening.

Douăzeci Si Unu

Miya couldn't help the smile on her face as she drifted off to sleep, the little grunts she had heard from Micah as he confirmed their meeting was actually kind of cute. She wondered just how much work went into training and what they were training for. Did Micah have other things that he tended to or was it just a bunch of goofing around? Not to mention she recalled he had said something, she thought, about hunting – what did they hunt? Was it humans? Animals? Was it just for survival or was there sport to it? Her mind buzzed frantically with so many questions that she wanted to remember to ask tomorrow. Miya hoped that they could get started on a better foot. As the night wore on though, Miya drifted off into a deep sleep. Torrents of images flashed behind her eyelids, some were beautiful and others were terrifying.

When the sun rose the next day, Miya sighed with a little relief. She wasn't sure if she could take another nightmare about a creature she had never known existed, but she was trying to quell her fears. Today she decided to go in with an open mind, especially after seeing her mate's parents interacting. The whole thing didn't seem too bad, but she had been wrong before. Miya chose a deep blue thin long sleeved shirt with a black tangtop underneath, just in case she got too warm later on and paired her favorite dark washed jeans, though that was mostly to keep her legs safe from any insects that would try to bite her. On her way out she grabbed a pair of well-worn but comfy running shoes and her satchel that had a water bottle and a few snacks. Once the bag was secure on her hip she headed out for their meeting point.

~*~*~

Micah's exhausted brain slowly slipped him into a light sleep, his breathing shallow but he welcomed the relief of rest. He didn't even toss and turn like he normally would at night. Not to mention when the sun peeked over the horizon, he actually slept in for a bit. Usually he would be up an hour before the sun to start his pack duties, but today he had a date. 'A *date,*' that thought, caused him to pop into a sitting position on his bed. He had a date with his mate. With a smile plastered across his face, he slipped from his bed to trifle through his closet to find the perfect outfit. It took some time to even find something that was clean enough to wear. Generally, the pack didn't care about smell or being dirty, it just reminded everyone of the earth but Micah wanted to look nice for his mate.

Eventually finding the right outfit, Micah bounded down the stairs in search of his father this time. It had been a while since his last haircut, so now was as good of a time as any. Not to mention, the full moon was just around the corner and he didn't want to look like some shaggy stray dog and he wanted to look good for Miya.

"Thanks dad," he called over his shoulder when they were done and started out the back door of the house so no one in the village would stop him and ask him what he was doing.

"Micah wait," his mother called to him and he groaned, he had hoped to get out of the house before his mother caught him. "It's nothing fancy. Just a couple of drinks and sandwiches with grapes," she told him and handed him a small wicker basket. He stared down at the basket, then at his mother, who had that knowing look on her face. Micah didn't really want to tote around a basket, hell he could just see the look on Miya's face of him trotting up to her with a basket in his jowls. He really wanted to tell his mother that it wasn't necessary, but one more look at her beautiful face and he lost his nerve.

"Thanks mom," he said, trying to be nice and gave her a kiss on the cheek.

Micah quickly ran towards the meeting place with the basket in his mouth and trying not to jar the basket too much as he took several turns. He couldn't help himself however, and jumped down a hill before coming to the river. Micah stopped briefly to catch his breath, turning his eyes towards the sun. It was getting late in the morning and Miya's scent was nowhere close. He lowered his head and shook it a little bit before getting to his paws. He knew that it would be easier for him to find Miya than for her to find him and thus he took off running again to track his mate.

~*~*~

Miya was thankful that the bugs weren't biting right now, as he walked along the river. Her eyes were watchful of the path and trees, she wanted to see if she could catch Micah before he saw her, but she was sure that she was going to fail in that endeavor because wolves had a great sense of smell but points for trying, right? Her long dark hair was pulled up in a bun that was now starting to uncurl and hung just below her neck. Miya was starting to work up a sweat just walking and then she heard a yip behind her.

Micah chuckled in his head when he stopped before his mate. The girl was hard to miss out in the forest with that strong sweet smell of honeysuckle wafting through the air and leading Micah right to his mate. He was glad though that Miya had seemed to be heading in the right direction and soon he yipped happily coming up behind her and then sat on his hunches as she turned around bringing that lovely scent flying directly at him.

"Glad you found me. I thought I took a wrong turn at some point" she said as a smile slowly lit up her face. "Did you cut your fur?" She asked, looking him over and recalling the last time she had seen the large white wolf and the image she had before was a completely terrifying beast you would see in a horror movie yet sitting before her now just looked like an oversized dog. She started to reach out, wanting to see if his fur was as soft as it looked, but quickly pulled her hand back. "Would you like to change so we can talk?" She asked though knew that he wouldn't exactly be able to answer in this form, though part of her wanted to study the transformation with her own eyes at some point. *'Maybe another time,'* she thought and watched Micah set the back down at her feet before ducking into some large bushes.

Once done, Micah brushed his hands over his clothes and returned to the path with Miya. "To answer your question, yes, I cut my fur...well actually I cut my hair but it sort of...well translates to fur in wolf form...if that makes sense." Micah explained as he stopped in front of Miya and snatched the basket off the ground once again. "My mother's idea of trying to be helpful..." he said, lifting the basket up before dropping his arm back down to his side. "She packed us a small lunch," he finally said and then motioned that they could start walking if she wanted to.

Douăzeci Si Doi

Her eyes watched Micah pick up the basket before laughing softly at the explanation for it. "That was kind of her to make us lunch. Why don't we eat it by the river?" She stated as they began to slowly walk down the path and further into the forest.

"That sounds like a brilliant idea." Micah confirmed and was holding back a little flicker of hope for the moment.

"So...I've been feeling a little guilty...how's your shoulder doing?" She tentatively asked, touching her own shoulder that mirrored the injury, she didn't feel the pain anymore from that day, so she wanted to make sure that Micah was ok and not drugged up on painkillers or something. "I won't exactly apologize for doing it because when a bunch of wolves are chasing after you, humans tend to panic," she said, giving a nervous chortle.

Micah's smile faded a bit at the mention of his shoulder, only the pain of knowing his mate had done it to him remained, but the physical pain had gone a while ago. "My shoulder's doing fine. I never did thank you for patching me up...so thank you," he said briefly. "I wouldn't expect you to apologize for it, nice to know that my mate can handle herself, even if the odds are stacked against her." Micah said, his smile returning a little bit and happy that the moon hadn't settled him with some weakling. "Oh and before I forget, I suggest that you invest in some kind of large bottle of painkiller or something because with the full moon just around the corner there is going to be a lot going on in the pack." He remembered glancing at the calendar in the kitchen that morning before taking off. Every member of the pack always made sure of the date, so there were no surprises because things always got testy between everyone at the full moon.

Miya was glad that Micah understood the position she was in when they first met, though her brows soon creased when Micah mentioned the moon. He seemed particularly rattled by the matter. "What's so special about the full moon? Why would I need painkillers? Are you getting into a fight?" She asked, her voice full of worry and confusion.

"Well, fights can happen and generally everyone in my age group likes to challenge me, but it's mostly out of fun. That's not exactly what I'm referring to," Micah explained a little, sensing something off about Miya's tone. Micah noticed that Miya had stopped walking to stare at him, so he stopped as well and turned towards her with a deep breath.

"At the full moon it's not going to be mortal combat or anything, but it can be quite vigorous. High emotions, intense situations, fur, biting...I'm sure you get the picture. Most feel the urge to get into a brawl more than normal and, being the strongest in my age group, they like to challenge me. I'm not usually one that backs down either," he explained and watched as Miya bobbed her head that she understood. He just knew that she would catch onto that bit since he had already tried to pick a fight at a bar.

"So painkillers, got it. Anything else?" She said while shifting to start walking again.

Micah pursed his lips; he wasn't sure if he wanted to tell Miya about the other little thing that happened at the full moon. *'It could be taken the wrong way. Miya might think that I'll hunt her down and rape her or something.'* He thought and then quickly shook his head no. "Nope, nothing else," he confirmed and they began to walk again.

This was going to be the first full moon with his mate and it seemed a little more thrilling to him, but Miya could get scared even worse. "Well...OK, yes, I suppose there is one other matter, um...the reason I told you to get some more painkillers was because I think I'm going to fight the transformation...you see, when the moon is full and hanging low in the sky, it's hard not to shift. Almost like the moon is calling us to return to our roots and rejecting that call is painful, but it would be less painful than all the brawls I would get into and then there are others that will....well, anyways, that's enough of that. What would you like to talk about?" Yep, he chickened out on telling Miya about all the mating that would be going on in the open along with all the sounds that would emit from his pack's lovemaking, but it wasn't like he was lying to her – just omitting certain things.

Miya was glad that it didn't seem like things during the full moon would be that terrible, but she did make a mental note to stop at the drugstore for some painkillers and maybe Epsom salt. However, Miya almost stopped dead in her tracks again. "Micah, don't do that. If this is something that is normal, then please just go with the flow like you normally would. I don't want this...what we..." she sighed, trying to make her thoughts more coherent, "what I'm trying to say is that you shouldn't put yourself through unneeded pain, so please promise me you won't do that and don't worry about me. I'll be just fine. I'm tougher than I look," she huffed out and touched Micah's arm just to show that she meant what she said. Micah glanced over at Miya and could see the intensity in her eyes and it sparked a primal need in him. He eyes glazed slightly, her words lost on him at the moment, since he was thinking about how sexy Miya looked right now and how he would like to pick her up, throw her over his shoulder and find a place off of the path that he could push her down to have an amazing round of sex in the tall grass.

"Micah?" Miya tapped his arm once again and pulled him from his daydream.

Micah quickly wiped the thoughts from his head and cleared his throat. "Sorry. I'll just see how things are going before making a decision about transforming or not. So what about you? What would you like to discuss?" Micah asked once again, trying to change the subject so his lustful brain would stop coming up with different scenarios of him ravishing his mate. Miya jerked at Micah's quick retort,

"Well, I wanted to fix things. After having some time to think things over, I don't think it would be so bad for us to...connect I suppose." She stated simply as they came up to the river and found a decently comfortable spot to relax.

Douăzeci Si Trei

Micah could almost feel himself throwing logic and rationality out the window to feel that connection and satisfaction one got from engaging in a session of love-making. Not to mention he wanted Miya to feel what he felt for her and show her that he was not just the big bad werewolf human's told their children. "So if we are going to start over I guess we should talk about a few things...the main one I want to talk about is, I don't like that you are so trusting of other guys...or rather any guy for that matter. I know that sounds strange coming from me, but I just can't help the fact that I still think you should have let me pound that Jason guy into a bloody pulp." Micah told Miya, though the scary part was that his tone remained calm, almost an eerie calm, but he was trying not to let his emotions bounce around too much around Miya.

Miya was happy when Micah agreed to start over, but when he brought up the topic of Jason and other guys she patted the grass next to her. "I stopped you because it would not be a fight, there would be no honor in you beating up the guy that could never be able to fight back against you. To me, that is just bullying. I stopped you because, not only is Jason one of my only friends, but because I already knew you would win and there would be no victory, just a big guy knocking down a smaller guy." She said, recalling her own high school life of torment and how bad bullies could be. "I was bullied as a kid, and I hated the idea of you turning into that so I asked you not to. I was happy that you listened but you lost the high ground when you struck him once." She said, patting Micah's shoulder. "As for the conversation of me with other guys, I don't understand what you mean by 'to trusting'. It's not like they are going to jump me and force me to have sex with them. Not only is it against the law, but it is also morally wrong." She stated while also thinking the mate thing could possibly be causing Micah to be over territorial right now.

Micah had to prevent a growl from escaping his lips; he didn't want to beat the guy down for honor or a victory. He wanted to teach the horny little bastard a lesson, but if that was how Miya saw it, then there was nothing more for him to say. However, that didn't stop him from thinking of so many other things that he could say. "You say that your friends wouldn't force you to do anything. Yet Jason forced a kiss on you. To me, your judgment is off," Micah said with a shrug of his shoulders. Now his sarcastic and rude behavior was coming out, so it wasn't the best idea to talk about the jerk from last night, but it had bugged Micah. "Besides, it wasn't like I wouldn't give the fucker a fighting chance. I would just make sure that he couldn't get out of bed for a few days." Micah said nonchalantly, he knew that humans couldn't take the beating like his own kind could and he was not about to ruin his perfect record of never killing a human because of one stupid human or because his mate was too naive to see how attractive she was. "We should probably move on to another subject, otherwise we are just going to piss each other off," Micah stated and pulled his hands behind his head to lay back into the lush grass, staring up at the sky for a minute before closing them.

Miya's heart was beating roughly, easily distracting her as Micah's smell finally drifted in her direction. She closed her eyes, enjoying his strong scent of vanilla and vetiver. Micha was doing the same thing, he was memorizing Miya's scent, feeling it right down to his core, but unfortunately, he could also smell other wolves in the area. Most likely watchers that his father sent to keep an eye on him, they were pretty far off, so he didn't bother hunting them down at this moment. Instead, Micah focused on

Miya and everything about her.

Douăzeci Si Patru

Miya felt the small hairs on the back of her neck rise, like something out of a horror movie just before the murderer kills you. She took a deep breath to get the heavy feeling in her chest to ease and then set her sights directly on Micah. "Jason didn't force me to kiss him, he kissed me and I pushed him off and he stayed off. He thought I was into him but I corrected that, so violence was not needed," she sternly explained. It was still a bother to her that Micah went straight into violence. She knew that men usually went that route, but even then most human males would at least think about what they were going to do...or at least she hoped in her heart. Those thoughts made her wonder, since Micah was a werewolf, if that was yet another difference between Micah and humans.

"I would hope that you'd give him a chance, but I also know that you would not lose. I know that and you know that. Fighting someone you know is weaker than yourself is just bullying. It made me happy though that you proved you could take the high road." She said softly, moving so she was sitting closer to Micah, feeling strangely better once her hip brushed against the other. Miya was about to bring up another point, but as Micah suggested they move onto a different topic, she bit her lip in thought.

"Alright, how about we talk about what we are going to do about being 'soulmates.' I never thought I would get into a relationship after I left home but I find myself wanting to now. So my question is, would you like me even without this bond? Is it only the bond that makes you like me?" She asked, averting her eyes.

The more time she spent with Micah the more she found herself pulled to him and wondering if he actually liked her and if so, what exactly did like about her. She began to worry that Micah was only looking at her because of the bond. What if there was no bond? Would she just be another weak and pathetic human to him, one of many in a mob?

Micah was taken aback by the subject Miya changed to; this subject wasn't one he would have chosen but he supposed it was something that, as a human, Miya had to ask. But for Micah, there was nothing better for him to fight for; the bond was all that mattered to wolves, aside from protecting family. Micah could sense there was more lying in Miya's words than what she asked and he wondered if there was something she was fishing for.

"The bond is there to help us find our mate. It's not something that forces two people together. If the pull wasn't there, I would still have found you and wanted you...it would just have taken longer. You may not have been my first choice of what I wanted, but it's more about what we need, though I will have to say your good looks are a plus and your personality is intriguing, at times infuriating." Micah took a small short breath after his long-winded explanation right before yawning into the back of his hand. With the sun beaming down on them and his short run earlier, Micah was feeling a bit sleepy but that was probably because he was lacking energy. "So my question to you - what do you mean when you say 'what are we going to do about being soulmates' question, what did you mean by that? It's not like there is anything that we can do about it...I mean you can straight up reject me, move away and try to hide, as well as I could have pushed the feeling of connection away, telling myself that it was all in my head or we both can accept it. But the bond and pull will still always be there. However, I'm still curious as to why you are so willing to be around me now...you know, since I scare you and I'm nothing but a caveman, because to tell you the truth, I don't care to change who I am just." Micah flat out told

Miya. He figured it was better to be honest up front from now on, so the rate of misinformation was minimal.

Miya blinked when Micah said that the bond was to find, and not to force love onto the two people. That information made her feel ten times better, but the best thing she heard was when Micah said that he would still search for her, with or without the bond. She felt a flush crawl up the back of her neck. "And what's so infuriating about my personality?" She challenged him with a smile on her face.

Micah chuckled in response, "that right there. You are not afraid to speak up or question even though you are human. Even some other Weres don't even have those kinds of guts."

Miya's smile grew at Micah's explanation about her personality. She had been terrified before, but after getting to know Micah and his family, they didn't seem any different than your average person – the only difference she could see was that they could shift into an animal. Miya, though, shook her head when Micah mentioned that she could run, but that thought only made her think of her family. She'd already run from them, and she wasn't about to run again, especially from someone willing to call her 'soulmate.'

People look all their lives for their soulmate, and hers came out of nowhere and picked her up saying that she was his wife already. It was cute now that Miya looked back, and after seeing how Micah's mother and father acted she felt less nervous, not to mention all the love there. "I don't want you to change; I think you're cute after looking back at it all. I was scared because things like this never happen to me." She said softly before shifting to lie on her side staring at Micah. "I've run so much in my life already. I'm pretty much run out. I am willing to give this soulmate thing a shot if you are still OK with a human, but if my father ever comes by, you cannot harm him in any way, shape or form, even if he hurts me. He's my father after all." She warned him with a curt sigh. "Want to eat your mother's food?"

She asked, smiling softly as he looked up at the sky.

Douăzeci Si Cinci

Micah bolted upright from the spot he was lying on to glare at Miya. "And why can I not hurt the man if he hurts my mate? No one should have the right to cause my mate pain. I don't care if they are family. Family should never do that to one another!" Micah exclaimed, disregarding the question about food. He couldn't believe that Miya would even tell him something like that and then say there was nothing he should do about it. Micah might have agreed if Miya had asked him to try not to hurt her father, but Miya had straight up told him that he couldn't do a damn thing to protect his mate.

Miya jerked slightly at Micah's outburst, flinching a little as the man's voice rose higher and angrier. She wasn't trying to anger the guy, but it was just something that she wanted to be honest about. Her eyes softened, remembering to keep her cool so things didn't blow up yet again. "It's a cultural difference. My parents are Russian, they both believe in pushing their children until the breaking point for them to get far in life. That's why I ran away as soon as I turned 18, and that's why I have not spoken to them since. I just wanted to give you a heads up, if you were to ever...I don't know how, but if you met my parents." She said, sighing softly while thinking back on how she was punished and pushed to reach her best. "I don't exactly see you meeting them at any point anyways so how about we drop this subject too?" She inquired, trying to lighten the mood again.

'Wrong answer,' Micah thought to himself and eyed Miya. His parents had smacked his hands as a child to make sure he didn't ruin his appetite or push him to train, but he could handle it. It was not right for Miya's parents to hurt their own daughter just to make her better. That thought ticked him off greatly.

"I'll let it go for now, but not forever," he sternly told her and Miya just groaned with a shake of her head.

"Alright. So food?"

"I suppose a bit of food would be good," he said, and his mood finally switched, but his eyes still burned with anger, though his stomach was quickly starting to trump everything else. He was sometimes the true definition of a boy and dog, though he hated to admit it.

Miya was relieved as soon as Micah's mood seemed to improve. She opened the basket and fished a couple of sandwiches and fruit out for them. "Please thank your mother for me when you get home, it was so nice of her to pack us a lunch," she said, smiling. She knew that they would end up talking about a few things again, but until then, she wanted to enjoy their day and was happy to find out that food was a good distraction. Micah nodded in response to Miya, and that he would tell his mother that she had thanked her for the food. He took a few grapes and popped them into his mouth, enjoying the sweet burst of flavor before swallowing and, with a burst of confidence, picked Miya's hand up.

"I would really like this to work out and I will promise to try not to kick the hell out of other guys you talk to, but I cannot and will not stand by, if your father hurts you. That's the last that I'll say on the matter for the time being," Micah stated, since he couldn't exactly keep his mouth shut on the matter. This also was not just him being overprotective, but this was his love for her...well and maybe a bit of the impending full moon.

Miya stared down at her hand clutched in his with a smile until Micah spoke and she wanted to groan even louder, but she also knew that this was how he was. "I guess I can live with that, but they are my parents and as much as they were hard on me.

I still don't think I could stand the thought of seeing them hurt. Even if it was to protect me," Miya explained, even as she saw the affection shining through his eyes and that was sweet, but she needed him to understand this. "I appreciate the sentiment though, Micah," she said, gripping the other's hand a little before letting it go so the man could eat his food.

Micha's eye twitched, he was being serious and she seemed to brush him off again. *'New plan,'* he thought, and turned to his sandwich. "You should just come live with me in my village. I will deal with everything they have to throw at me, but I don't exactly like hearing about you being pushed until you break..." Micah told Miya. He was beginning to like the idea of his mate coming to live with him rather than her staying in the human world.

Miya's eyes widened and she choked on a grape with Micah's statement. "Oh no, I don't think so. I can't live there. Well, not until after I get my job, then maybe I can think about moving. Next topic," She exclaimed once she stopped coughing.

He knew that his offer to have Miya live with him wouldn't go over so well, but he could at least try and he wasn't going to give up on the issue. He would have Miya live with him no matter what, it was just customary for the wife to live with her mate and leave their pack, so it shouldn't be any different with Miya. "Nope. I'm not giving up on this one", Micah told her matter-of-factly before taking another bite of his sandwich and relaxing back on the grass.

Miya laughed when Micah said he was not going to give up on the matter of living arrangements. "Well then it's a good thing I'm stubborn too. As I said, not until I think I am ready and only if these little get-togethers work out." She said with a cheeky smile and then pulled out a water bottle from the basket and took a swig.

Douăzeci Si Sase

Miya turned and looked up at the sky. "Alright, since we've talked about the pack and some about my family...why don't we take a walk around town and get to know each other more. I feel like I am being watched here," she said, scratching the back of her neck, and then stood up. Micah followed suit and got to his feet as well.

"Sounds good to me."

"Mind stopping by my place real quick? I'd like to grab a few things," she said smiling, picking up the remaining food and trash and putting it back into the basket to be thrown out later.

"I'm fine with stopping by your place...gives me a chance to see where you live," Micah said with an evil but playful smile on his face and snatched the basket from the ground, placing it on a nearby bench. He didn't want anything weighing them down and, besides, if his little babysitters really wanted something to do, then they could take it back to the village for him.

Miya eyed Micah when he showed off his evil but playful smile. It was cute to see, but at the same time she wasn't sure what the guy was planning. "I don't even want to know what you are planning, Micah," she said, laughing a little and watching as Micah winked at her.

"People always feel like they are being watched in the woods, too many horror films I say," Micah said with a smile on his face and then slung an arm around Miya's shoulders to steer her back towards town. She flinched when Micah threw his arm around her shoulders but quickly relaxed and gave Micah a smile, not hating the gesture.

"Well, I guess you're right, it just creeps me out. Just the thought of someone watching you gives me the shivers. Not like the city; there are too many people to really watch them." she said, shaking her head as they headed towards town, which confused her. "Shouldn't we take the basket back to your mother; does she not want it back? It's not good to litter," she said, looking up at Micah as they pushed onwards.

Micah waved her concerns away. "It'll be fine. I'll swing back later and grab it", he told her, and was happy that it seemed like she bought his white lie. When he was sure that Miya wasn't paying attention, he quickly looked over his shoulder to the dark parts of the trees, pointed to the basket and mouthed 'take this back please' before turning back to the path ahead of them.

~*~*~

The town was crowded, people out and about for the weekend and moving from shop to shop. Luckily, it didn't take long for Micah and Miya to get to her apartment and Miya started to lead him to her front door. Miya pulled out a key from her pocket and unlocked the door, but then quickly stepped in front of Micah before he could walk inside.

"Before you say anything, I have two roommates. They're not here at the moment. One is a guy and the other is a girl. They often have other's over to drink, party and other activities. I'm just warning you now, seeing as how you like to continually 'sniff' things and I don't need you going alpha on me right now," Miya explained, and then stepped inside with enough room for Micah to walk in as well.

Micah squinted his eyes at Miya, not liking her words one bit, and walked further into the small living room.

"Make yourself at home, I'm just going to grab a few things from my room," she said with a smile and picked up the TV remote, tossing it at Micah before disappearing into her room.

Douăzeci Si Sapte

Micah was not impressed with Miya's warning, nor the fact that one of her roommates was a guy, but he didn't have enough time to comment when she threw the remote at him. Micah growled very loudly as his eyes wandered around the place and, like Miya had said, he began to sniff the area. He wanted to get a better sense of Miya's roommates and if there was anything that he had to worry about, maybe even try to find something that would lead him to where her roommates mostly hung out at. However, he made sure that Miya didn't know what he was up to. Micah snooped around a little bit, getting sidetracked a couple of times and started going through things.

"You and your roommates don't engage...with each other, do you?" Micah questioned, feeling his possessive side rising quickly.

Miya probably laughed a little too hard at Micah's inquiry about her and her roommates. She knew that he was going to take her words the wrong way. *'Why not have a little fun,'* she thought to herself and poked her head out of her room, and saw Micah slowly moving through the living room doing his sniffing thing. "Well yeah, we engage...sometimes, when I see them," she told him in her most serious monotone that she could muster without laughing. Though, when Micah stopped dead in his tracks at her words, she could have sworn that she saw fur rising on the back of his neck.

"You what?!" He called, his tone more menacing than she thought it would be.

'*Touchy*,' she thought, and walked out of her room in a new outfit since she had sweated a little too much for her liking earlier and also grabbed her wallet. "Calm down killer," she laughed lightly and walked up to him. "I was only joking. I'm hardly either of my roommate's type. The most we do is talk every so often, but other than that, I keep out of their way and they stay out of mine."

Micah took a deep breath, his heart slowing down and he had to prevent himself from fully changing on the spot. "Not a very funny joke. Have you forgotten the bar event?" He questioned her and tried not to come off as pissed.

"Right, right," she agreed and gently pulled him by his arm back towards the front door. Miya dragged Micah from her place and made sure that everything was locked up tight once again.

Micah let Miya pull him from the apartment, still pretty peeve, not to mention he wasn't done snooping around, but he also didn't want to start an argument. "This is another matter you're going to make me let go, huh?" He questioned after she turned to look at him. Miya gave a tight smile and shook her head, yes. Micah sighed heavily, "got it," he said, and motioned for them to start heading towards the main street so they could continue their conversation. Micah actually could care less about looking around at the shops unless Miya wanted to buy something. He just couldn't wait for the moment he could spoil the girl rotten and tip things in his favor at some point.

"Well, where were we...ah, getting to know each other. What's your favorite color? Are there any special food dishes you like?" Micah started off. Those were some of the most basic questions he could think of. Oddly enough, not that he would admit it, but the answer did matter to him. He wanted to know anything and everything he could about his mate and his curiosity was already building up for the answers to the many questions bouncing around his mind.

Miya tilted her head at the questions, basic and simple, which confused her. "My favorite color is green, and I love this beef stew that my mom used to make. I have a slow cooker. Maybe I could make it for you and your family sometime." She said, smiling at the wolf before stopping in front of a bookstore. "Mind if we go in? I want to see if they have any new books." Micah gave a quick nod of his head just before they headed into the store. "Why don't you tell me your favorite color and favorite dish? Also, what is the number one thing you enjoy doing with your free time?" Miya retorted and began moving about the aisles.

Micah kept close to Miya watching the small little twitches of her face as she talked and he couldn't help but think how adorable she was. The way her nostrils flared when she took a breath or even the way that she walked, all of it called out to him. Micah shoved his hands into his pockets so he wouldn't have the urge to pull Miya to him and hold her there. He made a note of Miya's answer to his questions, quickly opening his mouth to ask a few more, only to close it when he was asked some questions.

"Well, my favorite color would have to be burnt red. I'm not sure why, but I find it beautiful. For my favorite dish...that's kind of a hard one. Can't go wrong with meat so long as it's rare or medium rare, but I also enjoy a few sweet items too." He said, shrugging his shoulders. Micah's eyes tracked everyone in the store all up until he saw the sign indicating the novels about werewolves and fought the urge to thumb through a few of them. Instead, he steered away from that section and walked up behind Miya, leaning down near her ear with his lips just a breath away from touching her. He had no intention of making the girl freak out, but his answer about his free time was something that shouldn't be heard by others. "In my free time, I enjoy basking in the sun or swimming while in my fur," he explained and then pulled back to look at another shelf of books. "How do you feel about extreme sports? Like cliff diving or bungee jumping?" Micah continued with his questions.

Douăzeci Si Opt

Miya blushed when she felt Micah come up behind her; she could feel the heat against her back and a ghost of his breath on her ear when he talked. Miya could understand why he had come so close to answer her question about what he liked to do since it involved some wolfy fun. She shook off the goosebumps until Micah asked about extreme sports, and the goosebumps were right back. "Oh no. No, not at all. The only extreme spots I would be willing to try would be parachuting, hang gliding or something I can grip on to for dear life, I'm not all that brave," she said laughing lightly and moved towards the science fiction novels.

She kept part of her attention on Micah and watched him look around but could see there wasn't really much interest in his eyes. "Are you into those extreme sports? Just thinking about cliff diving..." she shivered a little and pressed her shoulder against his a little before pulling back. "Just not for me, but I do like swimming. Maybe we both can sometimes. There are some lakes in the forest we could go to."

"It's too bad you don't like extreme sports, I'll have to think of something else then. Some of my buddies and I cliff dive every now and again, and I also skydive on occasion. I guess it has something to do with the adrenaline since it's hard to find things that get my blood pumping," he explained to Miya, letting one of his hands slip from his pants pocket to slip into Miya's. He wanted something to give him the feeling that Miya was actually his, since she wouldn't let him do much more. "You know...you could also hold onto me and cliff dive..." Micah offered up with a twinkle in his eye, but Miya turned a very telling look onto him, and he closed his mouth.

"I don't think so. Next" she said, and Micah sighed heavily.

"Alright. Swimming does sound nice for another date, " he said softly as they walked from the store, and Micah steered Miya towards the other side of the street.

Miya was shocked that she didn't feel weird about holding hands with Micah; in fact, it made her feel safer and happy. "So when's your birthday?" She questioned as they wandered down the sidewalk looking through windows of stores. "Mine's December 15th," Miya announced and started to swing their hands back and forth. She almost felt like they were in a romantic movie. Micah tilted his head at the birthday question. He thought he had mentioned something about the origins of his birthday a while back, but he could have been wrong, so he just shook it off. He did, however, file away Miya's birthday date so he could remember to get something for her when it came up.

"My birthday will be on the full moon this weekend, October 31st. Not that it's that big of a deal," he said with a small nod of his head and then started to head towards a store that he noticed Miya looking at.

"Really?! You'll have to show me what you would like for your birthday, " she said, smiling at him and bouncing a little bit at the thought that she would get to spoil someone. "How about you pick a shop and tell me something you would like for your birthday?" She said, turning away from the shop they had been moving towards.

Micah chuckled just at the sight of seeing how excited Miya got and wondered if he should tell her that the only thing he wanted for his birthday was her but thought better of his own words. "Don't worry about getting anything for me," he said softly and headed back towards the store he was originally going to take her into. Micah would rather find something to get Miya instead of the other way around.

"You know, with your birthday so soon, I could make that stew for you and bring it to your place as kind of a birthday present…" Miya stated, and pulled Micah into the store. She still wanted to actually get him something that he could keep with him or, at the very least, put it somewhere where he would see it all the time.

Micah's eyes widened. It would be an extremely bad idea for Miya to drop by the village on the night of the full moon. "You really shouldn't do that…y-you can just give it to me later. Really, my birthday isn't that big of a deal, and besides, you won't even be able to get near the place on that day, so don't even try." Micah told her rather frantically but sternly. It wasn't that he feared for Miya's life if she came…ok, yeah he did but he also didn't want to hurt her and rape her because the moon would be driving him nuts. "Well, I should be headed back home before the others worry too much, and you should get back too before I kidnap you again." Micah said with a chuckle, trying to change the subject even though it had actually crossed his mind.

Miya jumped at Micah's sudden change in demeanor and then pouted when he pulled her from the store. 'Home? Already?' She thought while they were walking back towards the forest. "Hold it!" She called a little louder than she had meant to and just noticed they were already out of town and very near campus once again. "I am your 'mate', so I should be allowed to see you on your birthday," she said, poking him in the side.

"Whoa, watch it there pointy fingers," Micah said, chuckling. "Really Miya, there's just going to be a small family get-together. Nothing spectacular, but if you would like, we can do something the day after," he offered, hoping to get Miya to change her mind.

Miya eyed Micah for a little bit. She had a feeling that he was trying to avoid telling her something and something that seemed pretty critical, but she shrugged her shoulders. She was sure that he would tell her in time. "Alright, but next time you tell me what's really going on and it wouldn't be kidnapping this time if I said it was ok," she said with a cheeky laugh letting Micah continue to lead her back to her apartment. Before parting ways, Miya gave Micah a kiss on the cheek this time before waving him off.

"Have a good night, and I hope to see you soon." Micah called to her before turning and bounding for the village.

Douăzeci Si Nouă

Micah had wanted to spend another day with Miya before the full moon came, but that didn't even come close to happening. His father had him running around the village to help others to prepare some basement rooms, if not rooms for their kids, so they didn't just go running anywhere when they shifted. While the other groups went about town securing loose items near houses and the hunters marked paths with certain scents, just in case a few people got it in their head to hunt.

Even on the day of the full moon, when he could feel the hairs on the back of his neck standing on edge, he was doing prep work. He and his hunting group went out to get food for everyone so his mother and the other cooks could prepare it for later. When the sun started to set, that was when Micah decided to lock himself in the house. A few people questioned him if he would be joining them but he had just walked past them as if he hadn't heard them. There was no time for him to explain what he had planned to do, not to mention he didn't want to answer any of their questions. He just wanted to get someone to secure himself so that he wouldn't hunt down Miya.

The further the moon rose in the sky, it intensified Micah's urge to change like normal. He was being called back to his roots by the goddess stronger than ever on the night of his twenty-fifth birthday, on a blood moon like the one he was born under. She called to him to revel in his alpha nature, but he ignored the call, staying in his room, and refusing to change even into a partial form. His body had broken out into a cold sweat, his hands gripping the blankets on his bed. Micah's music was blaring in hopes of drowning out the noises of fighting that had already begun or the mating sounds of those that loved to be watched while they fucked. Micah couldn't deny that he would love to be tangled in a heated sex session with his mate but that would ruin everything, so instead he lay on his bed with pain rising from his refusal to change.

"I won't do it. I won't hunt her down just because of instinct", he growled up to the moon that he currently couldn't see.

~*~*~

Miya hummed to herself, an old tune she had long since forgotten, but she was happy. Micah had told her that his birthday wasn't a big deal, but then again she wasn't really one to listen a lot of the time. She wanted to celebrate his birthday, she wanted to be near someone who actually enjoyed her presence. "Hope he won't be too mad," she murmured to herself as her eyes shifted down towards the decent-sized pot of stew she had made. The smell of her family's traditional stew was seeping from the lid and even making her own mouth water. 'Gotta concentrate' she thought to herself, and finally returned to scanning the woods. She really had wished that she had asked Micah how to get to his village before this night, though she never figured she would willingly come here. Her first experience was rather tasteless, to say the least. "It's different now," she announced to herself, even though her nerves were getting to her.

The forest was pretty dark by this point and there were several strange sounds in the air. Miya could have sworn she heard moaning at one point, but that soon was drowned out by growling and what she assumed was snarling and jaws snapping. She shook slightly as goosebumps covered her skin and she quickened her pace. Unfortunately, she only made it a few yards from the earlier noises before searing pain ripped from her toes to the top of her head and she almost dropped the pot of stew. Miya hunched over for a little bit just trying to breathe through the pain, *'DAMN! This is ten times worse than just some play fighting,'* she angrily thought, but even that only lasted a few seconds because Miya wondered just what Micah was doing that would be causing her this amount of pain.

Once the pain dulled, Miya continued her trek through the forest. This time she steered towards the noise that made the hair on her body rise and chanted to herself that the noises were just Micah and his family. It was the only thing she had to go off of, to find her mate's village and her luck paid off. She saw the back of Micah's house coming into her sights. "Finally, something familiar" she huffed out. She quickly walked up to the back sliding glass door before anyone else found her there and rapped lightly on the glass. "Micah?" She called out, her heart beating frantically because she knew she wasn't supposed to be here and hoping that Micah wouldn't be that furious at her. "Micah?" She called a little louder.

Treizeci

A spike of pain ripped through Micah, he was starting to lose the battle with himself and not a second later, he found himself on the floor. He really just wanted to give in and shift, but if he did that, then he would fully shift and force himself to run north. Away from the town so he could avoid using Miya for the urges he had. He took a deep breath while pawing at the tangle sheet that had come with him onto the floor. His nails lengthened and easily tore the fabric and he resisted the urge to gouge the floor. His mother would be pissed if she knew he had done that.

Unfortunately, Micha's plan didn't work when a breeze picked up, forcing all kinds of smells into his room from the scent of sex made by the pack to...

"Miya! Oh shit!" He exclaimed through his labored breathing. His mate hadn't listened to him and was here. *'How did she even find the place?'* He thought as another gust of wind blew into his room and forced him into a partial transformation to be compatible with his mate. After his breathing leveled out, Micah jumped to his feet, dashing towards his window. His eyes searched out for that familiar form and when his eyes landed on the human at the back door to the house, Micah vaulted out of his window to land behind Miya.

Miya had no time to react after seeing Micah pop his head out of a window, even her words stuck in her throat as she barely caught the sight of her mate jumping from the third story of the house. A split second later, Micah was at her back and the stew doused the back porch while her breath hitched in her throat. "I-I-I wwanted to at l-least give you s-s-something for your birthday. I know you t-told me not to make a big deal out of your b-birthday but..." she stammered while Micah pushed against her back and turning her head to the side while she talked to the half-wolf Micah. Damn, the man even looked mouthwatering in that half state, even if she couldn't understand why he was in this weird partial form.

"I told you not to come here tonight," he growled out, trying to contain the lust in his voice. He could not believe that his mate would do this to him and tonight of all nights, especially after he told her not to. Now his sex drive was violently shoved into overdrive, as well as being mostly naked aside from a loose pair of jeans that were kind of shredded now.

Micah grabbed Miya's arm as gently as he could, spun her around to face him and shoved her up against the side of the house. Miya squeaked with the sudden quick movement, her head spinning a bit before she could refocus on Micah's face. "I cannot be held accountable for my actions from this point on," he growled, which turned into a moan as he pushed himself up against Miya's body. Feeling that heat coming off of his mate was soon driving him over the edge and no matter how much he tried to contain himself it just made it worse. Every time the fur on his arms or legs grazed against Miya's body, he moaned with his eyes halfway closed.

Miya groaned in response to the other's bare chest and arms pressing against her own exposed arms. "Accountable? M-Micah?" She asked as Micah pushed against her more. She held still from the sound of the other's voice alone and shivered at the ideas it gave her. Miya snaked a hand up to press against the half-wolf Micah's chest, shivering when she felt the other's need against her pelvic bone.

'He's not thinking...outside...oh god!' Her mind whirled shortly before she looked around the backyard. She could have sworn at one point she saw another werewolf run by with what looked like another half-wolf female. It looked as though they were play fighting and licking each other. Her blush deepened and covered her ears and neck at this point.

Micah was sniffing and licking at Miya's neck himself at this point. Taking in all of his mate's scent and humming his approval, when he could smell her arousal enter the air as well. Though he did snort at Miya's excuse of his birthday, it still wasn't a good enough reason in his mind for Miya to use and come here. He really didn't want to reveal his primitive side to her since she had stated that he scared her not too long ago. However, the moon was making it difficult for him to think with each passing second and the pheromones that hung so heavy in the air were not helping either. Even hearing a few of his pack mates running by did not deter him from the path he was now on.

Treizeci Si Unu

Micah pushed his body up against Miya's even more now as a pair of lovers passed, their energy affecting him like crazy. Miya shivered when Micah pressed harder against her before the other was ripped away by a playful pack member. Miya was awarded a reprieve when Micah felt something barrel into his side. She shivered softly watching the wolves bounce around with energy, and talking about taking things inside. Miya would have loved to take whatever this was going to be, inside the house as well.

"Come on Mic! Where's your spirit?" Derek, one of the wolves that were present the day Micah found his mate, bounced from foot to foot. The guy was a few years younger than him but at times acted way below his age.

"Not now Derek!" Micah called out in a territorial growl, only to feel a hand on his shoulder.

"He didn't mean anything by it, Micah, and if you don't want others finding out about your cute little mate then I suggest you take her inside," Vin's voice came above the growls and watched as Derek's grin spread more.

"Oh come on, Vin. Can't we have fun with Mic like we used to, remember all the fun romps we had," Derek called out until Vin launched himself at the guy and drug him to the ground.

"Take your mating habits out of here!" Micah barked at them and quickly turned back to Miya.

It was a concern of his that others would run past the back of the house, but his reason was almost gone by this point. Why should he be concerned about what the pack thought of his mate? It was his mate, end of story and it wasn't like it would hurt the pack. He would still become Alpha and his mate could still bear his pups for the next generation.

Micah leaned his head down to Miya's neck, sucking in a deep breath, eliciting a deep moan from him before he pulled back. "You are wearing far too many clothes." He snarled out his displeasure. If his mate was moronic enough to go against his advice and come here anyway because of some stupid birthday, then he saw it as an open invitation. "I hope you have no plans of walking later," Micah partially warned and took the pleasure of snaking a hand under Miya's shirt and enjoying the feeling of the soft furless skin against his rough partially shifted hands. Slowly he moved his hand upwards and took Miya's shirt along with his movements until the garment was discarded off to the side. Micah would eventually get her naked but a small speck of his rational side was screaming at him to get Miya inside before going any further. Unfortunately, the wolf in him wanted to feel the moon on his back as he joined with his mate for the first time.

She shivered when Micah leaned down and moaned against her skin, and laughed nervously. She was told that she had too many clothes. "Sorry, I didn't think s-something like this was going to happen." Miya said before her eyes went wide as Micah took her shirt off. "Now who says I won't be walking later?" She asked cheekily before shivering at the feeling of those odd hands. Miya pressed her own hands against the other's half-furred form, stroking that soft black fur. She wondered if the moon also made Micah want to take her and Miya wasn't sure if this was a good step to take right now or not, but she wanted it.

"Is this the moon's doing?" She questioned, feeling a little insecure of Micah's feelings towards her. Miya understood that the bond was just to help Loup Garou find their mate, but what if Micah didn't really like her? What if the guy wanted her to stay away because he didn't want to have sex with a human? So many thoughts and what ifs were running through her head and she wasn't even sure if she could get any of the answers from Micah when he was like this. Miya slid her hands upwards towards the other's shoulder and pulled him down to her level and gave him a very deep kiss.

Micah snorted at Miya's words. How could she be asking such things right now? Did his mate feel nothing for him, especially when the moon was out? Or did all humans think this way? So negative. He was starting to get a little mad by this point; he could not believe that Miya would be questioning him at this point and when his body was in so much need for her. "If I wanted to just fuck something, then I would have sought out someone from the pack, but it was you, who pushed me to transform," he huskily told Miya while his head lowered to his mate's neck once again and tasted the flesh presented to him. "And I am the one who says you won't be walking later...unless you'd like to try and walk out of here. By all means, getting to catch you sends a thrill through me," Micah said as his voice dripped with lust and shifted about an inch away from Miya.

On any other night he would have loved to chase after Miya and tackle her to the ground, but tonight was different and his mate was already in front of him.

"Would you tell her already, jeez you two are making even me sick," Derek's voice sounded once more only to be quickly stifled and dragged off by Vin. Micah threw a look over his shoulder at the two and watched Derek lose color in his face while Vin mouthed an apology.

Micah turned to Miya, clasping both his mate's hands in one of his and pulled them above her head while his other hand snaked into her pants. "Seems like your body doesn't mind one bit, so why does your mind?" Micah questioned sweetly before returning to kissing Miya's neck and nipping at it lightly.

Treizeci Si Doi

Miya was happy to learn that this wasn't the moon doing this to him and that he was actually feeling something for her and she was for him as well. That scared her a little bit, to think that there was someone who could mean so much to her and that it wasn't just a fate bond or something like that, that made either of them feel like this. Miya became confused when Micah told her that she was the one to make him transform, she thought that was just a normal thing for his kind. "I pushed you to transform?" She questioned, her teeth clicking together as a soft breeze picked up and grazed across her exposed skin.

Micah gave a throaty chuckle, there were still a few things that he forgot to tell Miya...well, intentionally forgot to explain. He was still a little worried that if Miya knew what he went through on a daily basis, then she would get scared and run off for real. "Your scent drives me mad," Micah happily growled and snaked and hand further into Miya's pants, stroking her clit through her panties. Micah was happy to find that she was already soaking through her under garments, which further drove his lust.

Miya's breath caught in her throat at the mention of her running just so that Micah could catch her. It was an odd thing to say and the weirdest part – her own heart sped up at the thought, but there was no time for her to react when Micah pulled her hands above her head. "M-Micah....there are p-people right there," she stammered trying to be stern with him but her voice came out a lot huskier than she had planned. Micah shifted his face away from the crook of Miya's neck to gaze into her eyes, his eyes clouding more.

"All the more fun to have others watch, don't you think?" He questioned but wasn't really looking for an answer. He did, however, allow Miya's hands to drop down to her waist so he could use both his hands to unbutton and start to remove his mat's pants. Micah would try to hold out for as long as he could but the longer he dragged this out, the more his need grew, even his tail swished from side to side at a mad pace like a dog that was beyond excited to see his master. Miya bucked into Micah's touch and gave a soft moan of pleasure, even Micah's growling was starting to thrill her.

"Have them watch?!" Miya gasped.

"If you insist! Just let yourself go and stop thinking" Micah responded cheerfully and attacked Miya's right nipple, sucking and pulling at the sensitive flesh with his teeth. He watched the nub perk up and then gave the same treatment to the other nipple, just waiting to hear those beautiful sounds from his mate that others around them were already howling.

Miya threw her head back, another moan loudly escaping her lips with the assault on her nipples. She couldn't tell if it was hotter to have someone watching them or if it was just the fact that, for once, someone was solely focused on her. Micah's tail continued to swish back and forth, smacking Miya in the leg a few times and every time Micah ducked his head down, she could see the other's behind them. Every so often they would break from their own play and stare at them, which caused Miya's blush to deepen. "Oh god~ Micah~" she lustily called out. Miya's hand entwined in the fur of Micah's chest, gripping and releasing until Micah backed up a little. She stared at him confused and then he gently tugged her hand so she would step away from the house. Miya stumbled a little into Micah's chest, Micah was done talking. He scooped her up bridal style before turning to the middle of the yard and laid her down gently. He needed to get out into the expanse of the backyard, he wanted to bask in the moon with his mate. Micah was still trying to keep a bit of his head right now and not treat Miya like any normal Loup Garou, whom they would normally be slamming into each other and ripping at clothes and flesh a like.

'Human,' Micah reminded himself. "Take off your clothes and let the moon wash over you," he ordered. He could hold back his actions all he wanted, but with the full moon and the Alpha gene rising up to take over, it was getting harder to soften his voice.

"Micah! I didn't actually mean for others to watch," she cried out and Micah just smiled down at her. "Y-your parents might see."

Micah rolled his eyes, how many more excuses was she going to come up with? His patience was already wearing thin. "My parents are in the northern forest, besides it shouldn't matter," he groaned out an explanation. "Please Miya, just listen for once," he pleaded.

Miya glanced around the yard a little, noticing more glowing eyes showing up, and then grinned. "How about you take them off, Micah?" She said, challenging him. "Your tone isn't going to help you get your way with me," she then stated cheekily. Micah smirked; he loved it when Miya stood up to him. Not that she really stood a chance against him, but it was cute that Miya tried at least. He was becoming more aware of the reason why fate paired them together. Micah crouched down and quickly made away with the rest of Miya's clothes and his cock twitched in anticipation. "I will try to keep my tone in check, but since tonight is a full moon and my 25th birthday, the Alpha in me will come out more," Micah explained before gently pulling Miya's legs open. The last of Micah's resilience went out the window and his hands started to touch and caress any part of Miya's body that he could reach. His lips kissed every inch and licked whatever he could.

Miya gripped at Micah's shoulders, then his arms and then rested on his head as Micah moved further down until he was between her knees lapping at her core.

Treizeci Si Trei

Miya couldn't catch her breath, one moment she thought she was in time with Micah's tongue lapping at her and the next her head spun and she couldn't tell up from down. Her breath had long since gone ragged and only began to level once Micah began to work his way back up towards her lips. She hungrily kissed Micah once he was within reach and he returned the passion, their tongues dancing together as they exchanged everything including air. As Miya's mind returned to her, she had enough sense to wrap both her legs and arms around Micah and took the chance to roll them so that she was on top.

She grinned wildly down at Micah, a joyful chuckle erupting from her lips. "Happy Birthday Micah!" She announced, then leaned down, returning to kissing those taunting lips.

Micah rolled his eyes behind his eyelids at the happy birthday from Miya, yet again reminding himself that human's held birthday's higher than his pack did. The only thing Micah wanted right now, was to be deep inside his mate and to enjoy the pleasures of their mating session. However, Micah was slightly stunned when Miya rolled them so that she was on top, but as he stared up at that beautiful black hair shining in the moon, he wasn't too mad.

A few howls erupted in the air.

His hands reached up to caress the soft flesh of Miya's breast, squeezing them gently before pinching those perfectly perked nipples until he saw goosebumps spread down his mate's body. Micah ran one of his hands around Miya's ribs slowly, enjoying every inch of her flesh until his hand rested heavily on her back to hold her in place. He then captured one of her nipples between his lips; licking, nipping and sucking at the tender flesh. Micah's tail, on the other hand, had another idea as it snuck pass his legs to come up behind Miya and then Micah rocked his hips a bit so that his mate would be hovering over him, almost horizontally, so that his tail could start probing at Miya's heated entrance.

Miya gasped when she felt the fur of Micah's tail touch her core and couldn't even think of the words to scream at Micah for his odd attack.

"You're the sneaky type, aren't you," Micah mused as he grinned up at his mate who gave him a peck, but Micah engulfed Miya's lips in a heated and much needed kiss, making both their hearts race more.

Micah felt his tail becoming wet, knowing just exactly what was going on, and was glad that he pretty much had a third hand to help him. Micah couldn't wait much longer, his cock was growing painful and without any kind of release he would go mad and force himself inside his mate regardless of any protests.

"M-Micah?" She asked breathlessly before moaning when the tail breached her for the first time. Her walls tightened around Micah's tail and rocked her hips a little.

"Hold still, will ya. If you don't let me prepare you then it's going to hurt and I'd rather not do that to you if I can help it," he growled out, applying more pressure with his tail to the tight muscles of Miya's core, his arm squeezing a bit tighter so his mate wouldn't move and causing herself any unnecessary pain.

She shook her head a little at the order of sorts. "T-Then use your d-damn fingers~ ahh, t-the fur feels weird," she demanded while shivering and rolling her hips more, blushing at how she must look to everyone else at the moment. Miya felt like a horny teenager, unable to get into a room before jumping her kind of, sort of boyfriend. She gasped when she felt the other growl and felt Micah tighten his grip that forced her against that strong chest and then Micah's tail pressed harder into her. "D-Damn it~ Micah~" she exclaimed and did the only thing she could think to do at that moment; she leaned down and bit down on Micah's neck.

"Shit!" Micah called and gripped Miya's hair. He would have welcomed the bite on any other night but he hadn't expected his human mate to attempt something like that so soon. "Alright, I get it Miya," he said softly, as a purr like growl sounded in his throat. Micah pulled his tail from those tight muscles, letting it rest against the grass so that he could use his other hand, giving his mate what she wanted.

A bit reluctant to release his hold on Miya, he slid his hand down her back until his fingers found the now sopping wet folds between his mate's legs. Micah probed the entrance to test it, making sure his nails wouldn't hurt her. He had planned to take things slow but when Miya bit him all bets were off. Micah shoved two of his fingers into her cavity a few times until it softened.

It was probably still too soon but his cock was starting to pulsate painfully, he would make it up to Miya later. In a matter of seconds, Micah removed his fingers from his mate's body and pushed her towards the side and off of his chest. Micah then jumped at the chance to get behind her.

"Forgive me," he said softly, barely audible to the human ear most likely, but at the moment he wasn't too concerned about that. Micah gripped his cock and began to push himself into Miya's twitching hole. He was hoping that a human's body could adjust quickly like his species could, because the moment the head popped inside Micah thrusted all the way to the hilt, unable to control himself. Loud moans erupted from his throat every time he pushed himself inside his mate, while his claws dug into her hips to help him thrust better.

"Holy fuuuckk! Soooo good~" He moaned out and then felt Miya jerk forward as a lustful cry sang out from his mate. "Is this your good spot?" He asked, but not really looking for an answer. Micah angled himself and slammed harder repeatedly into that spot hoping to drive his mate insane with pleasure like she was doing to him.

Treizeci Si Patru

Miya shivered when she felt the tail slip from her body, and started to sit up to take a deep breath until she faintly heard Micah apologize for something. It seemed like she was losing bits of time every so often and her mind was having a hard time keeping up. At first her brows furrowed wondering what the guy was apologizing for and then the intense sensation of Micah's thick cock began to stretch her. Miya couldn't help herself and her back arched like she was a bow string being pulled tight.

"Breath."

She faintly heard Micah say and it took a second longer for her to actually get air into her lungs. The rush of air made her head spin more but it did relax her. It relaxed her to the point she felt a tingling sensation now and caused a moan to erupt from her lips. *'Was that me?'* She briefly thought before Micah thrust into her again and her world spun once more.

~*~*~

Micah watched every facial expression of his mate as she experienced something that he knew deep in his own core but even this time was different for him. He was finally sealing his bond with his mate. Micah couldn't understand how he went so long without this feeling, it was close to euphoria and what was even better - Miya wanted him as well. He could feel her tighten every so often, almost to the point he thought she was going to snap him in half but then the pleasure enveloped him and he would rock his hips at a faster pace.

Micah slipped partially into his own little world until he felt

Miya dig her nails in his back which caused a loud growl of satisfaction to emit from his lips. Once the wave of painful euphoria subsided a little he leaned down to lick at Miya's lips, tasting the tantalizing flesh once again. "You're driving me mad Miya." He murmured softly against her lips.

Miya on the other hand had begun moaning with each thrust into her and mumbling words that could not truly be understood. She was enjoying the blissful feelings sweeping through her and forgetting about everything around them. Miya greedily accepted the attention of Micah's tongue against her lips and parting her lips ever so slightly in hopes of a deeper kiss until he spoke. A flush crossed her face and she wanted to admit that he was driving her wild as well but Micah hadn't let up on his thrusting and all she could do was grind her head into the grass.

He could feel himself reaching his first climax at this pace, though he knew that it would only be the first of many and as his body tensed he gave way to the feeling. Micah lifted his head to the sky, letting out a howl that his semi-human form would allow and then fell forward, sinking his teeth into the soft flesh of Miya's shoulder, marking her as his mate for all to see. Miya screamed in response to the sudden teeth piercing her flesh as her fight or flight kicked in. Her mind was in a whirl, the pleasure enveloping her body and the pain radiating from her neck almost caused her to throw up. *'He's gonna kill me'* ran throughout her mind and stilled her movements in hopes that he would not actually kill her.

A few of Micah's group mates wandered near the sounds coming from Micah, sniffing the air and finally realized what was going on. Most of the others were fully shifted, having just got done with fighting while others were partially shifted like Micah. At the overwhelming howl from Micah, all in the area raised their heads as well and howled their approval of their next Alpha finally claiming his mate.

However Micah had stopped paying attention to the others by this point, feeling the pleasurable pain from the bite he gave Miya through their bond until he felt her emotion flip and when he tasted just the smallest hint of blood he pulled his head back. Panting heavily he studied Miya's face and she seemed petrified. *Fuck!* He called in his mind and slowly leaned down, giving Miya's trembling lips a kiss, "I won't hurt you, I swear it" he told her softly and watched her eyes as she stared up at him.

Miya could hear her heart beating in her ears as her body shook slightly. She broke out in a sweat and her body started to feel clammy as she stared up at the half-man half-creature. Miya tried to focus on the words spoken to her and more than that, tried to believe them. Micah could see the uncertainty in his mate's eyes but he could not take back what he had done. Yes, he should have explained to her what could happen if she came here but he was damn sure that she wouldn't pull a stunt like this.

"I will not hurt you ever. You are my mate, my one and true. This mark proves it, I promise that it was not done with ill intent" he told her as softly as he could through heavy breath. All movements had ceased as he just hovered above her and he carefully touched the fresh mark on her shoulder. "I hope that when you are ready you will leave the same on me," he told her and cupped one of her hands in his own and brought it up to the crook of his neck to show her what he meant. The whole time Miya's eyes shifted back and forth between Micah's eyes, trying to find any hint that he didn't mean his words.

Treizeci Si Cinci

Miya's mind was a whirlwind of emotions as she clung to Micah, her heart pounding in her chest. The world around them seemed to fade away as she buried her face into his chest, seeking solace in his embrace. Micah held her tightly, his touch gentle yet possessive, his warmth enveloping her like a protective shield.

As they laid in the grass, lost in their own private moment, the pack watched in awe and reverence. They understood the significance of this bond, the unbreakable connection that had formed between Miya and Micah. It was a rare and powerful union, one that would shape the destiny of their pack.

Micah sensed Miya's need for privacy so he scooped her up into his arms and with a swift movement, he leaped onto the awning protruding from his bedroom window, effortlessly carrying Miya in his arms. Without hesitation, he slipped inside, shutting out the world.

Inside the room, the atmosphere crackled with worry. Miya gazed at Micah, her eyes searching for answers, for reassurance. He met her gaze, his eyes filled with a mix of tenderness and longing.
"Miya," he whispered, his voice laced with emotion. "I never wanted to frighten you. I never wanted to hurt you. But this bond, it's beyond our control. It's a force that binds us together, forever."

Miya hesitantly nodded, her lips trembling as she found her voice. "I believe you, Micah. But it's overwhelming."

Micah reached out, caressing her cheek with his thumb. "We'll navigate this together, Miya. I'll be here every step of the way. We'll learn, adapt, and grow stronger."

With those words, Miya felt a flicker of hope ignite within her. She knew there would be challenges ahead, but she also knew that they had each other.

Micah gently guided Miya towards the bed, his touch conveying both tenderness and a hint of caution. She couldn't help but wonder if his sudden decision to sleep was a result of her being human. Doubts and insecurities began to cloud her mind, threatening to overshadow the connection they had just discovered.

As they settled under the covers, Miya couldn't shake the feeling that something was amiss. Micah sensed her unease and pulled her closer, his arms a comforting stronghold around her. "Miya, rest is essential for both of us. We can continue exploring our bond tomorrow."

Miya's heart fluttered at his words, uncertainty still present but somewhere inside she hoped that Micah was at least content with their bonding. She understood though that Micah's decision to prioritize sleep was not a reflection of her worth but rather a testament to his care and concern for their well-being. She nodded, silently agreeing to the much-needed rest.

As they lay side by side, their breathing slowly synchronizing, Miya finally understood the bond a little better, it wasn't just about mating; it was also about passion, understanding and support.

As the soft moonlight gently filtered through the window, casting a serene glow across the room, Micah and Miya lay side by side but Miya couldn't seem to sleep. Miya turned to face Micah, her eyes studying his sleeping face in the dimly lit room.

"Micah, what's going to happen? The pack, your future as Alpha? Our future?"

Micah's eyes snapped open, his gaze held a mixture of determination and tender affection. "It means that we'll face challenges, Miya, but we'll face them together."

Miya tried to keep the frown that threatened to cross her face, she wanted to believe that things were going to be like a fairy tale, cinderella or sleeping beauty with a happy ending but she was not so sure her story would have that since this was reality and not a fairy tale.

Micah leaned in, brushing his lips against Miya's forehead. "It's a lot to take in but we'll figure it out together."

"Micah, answer me honestly. The bond between us…what is the pack going to think? I'm human."

Micah's brow furrowed slightly, concern etched across his face. "Miya, a human-Loup Garou bond is uncommon, and not everyone will understand. But we should have hope. People fear what's different, but love has a way of breaking barriers."

Miya nodded, her gaze reflecting the turmoil of emotions within her. "I hope you're right, Micah. I don't want our bond to cause you trouble."

Micah brushed a strand of hair behind Miya's ear, his touch gentle and reassuring.

"Get some sleep Miya, we can talk more in the morning." Micah kissed her forehead and pulled the covers up before closing his eyes once again.

Cruel Dance of Fate

Book 2

Micah, a strong and destined future Alpha of the Firestorm Pack, has finally fulfilled his mate bond with Miya, a human handpicked by the moon goddess herself. Their joyous union, however, is short-lived as they face numerous trials and complications that threaten to tear them apart.

The primary challenge they encounter arises from within the Firestorm Pack. As news spreads of Micah's human mate, tensions rise among the pack members. Many question the decision to accept a mere human into their close-knit community, fearing the potential repercussions of such a union.

Struggling to find a balance between his loyalty to the pack and his love for Miya, Micah faces a difficult choice. Will he forsake his beloved mate to appease his pack's expectations, or will he defy tradition and fight for the right to be with the one he loves?

Meanwhile, the tensions intensify within the pack and disruptions threaten their unity. Just as Micah and Miya grapple with their internal conflicts, Miya's long-lost family suddenly resurfaces, seeking contact with her. Intrigued yet hesitant, Miya contemplates acknowledging her estranged family and potentially introducing her "boyfriend" to them. In doing so, she would reveal the hidden world of supernatural beings and the intricate social dynamics of the pack.

As Micah and Miya navigate this newfound territory, unsettling revelations come to light. Miya's family's true intentions become apparent, leaving her with a sense of unease and mistrust. Their agenda threatens not only Micah and Miya's relationship but also the stability of the Firestorm Pack.

With fate paying no heed to their desires, Micah and Miya

must navigate treacherous waters. They face challenges both within the pack and within themselves as they strive to find a resolution that satisfies both their hearts and their responsibilities. Can they overcome the external and internal pressures, or will their love falter under the weight of the trials they face?

In this dramatic tale of fantasy and romance, Micah and Miya's bond will be tested time and time again as they fight for their love, loyalty, and the future of their pack.

About The Author

A.r. Scritchfield

Based in the colorful mountains of Colorado A.R. Schrichfield is a genre- hopping writer with a passion for dramatic suspense, slow burning romance and cliffhangers.

As a mother of one she finds joy in the small moments- a simple smile, small victories at bedtime, and the sweet necter of the coffee bean.

With 10+ years of writing A.R. Schrichfield's characters live in her mind- they have backstories, hobbies, heck they might even pay their taxes! Come enter the mind of A.R. Schrichfield.... you won't be disappointed.